( Third Class Superhero

# ( Third Class Superhero

## Charles Yu

*A Harvest Original* ❀
HARCOURT, INC.

*Orlando*
*Austin*
*New York*
*San Diego*
*Toronto*
*London*

Requests for permission to make copies of any part of the work
should be submitted online at www.harcourt.com/contact or mailed
to the following address: Permissions Department, Harcourt, Inc.,
6277 Sea Harbor Drive, Orlando, Florida 32887-6777.

www.HarcourtBooks.com

Earlier versions of the following stories appeared in the following
magazines: "32.05864991%," *The Malahat Review;* "Autobiographical Raw
Material Unsuitable for the Mining of Fiction," *Alaska Quarterly Review;*
"Third Class Superhero" appeared as "Class Three Superhero,"
*Mid-American Review;* "Florence," *Eclectica;* "My Last Days As Me,"
*Sou'wester,* reprinted in the *Robert Olen Butler Prize Stories 2004;* "Problems
for Self-Study," *Harvard Review;* "Realism," *Mississippi Review;* "The Man Who
Became Himself," *The Gettysburg Review;* "Two-Player Infinitely Iterated
Simultaneous Semi-Cooperative Game with Spite and Reputation," *Eclectica.*

Library of Congress Cataloging-in-Publication Data
Yu, Charles, 1976–
Third class superhero/Charles Yu.—1st ed.
p. cm.
"A Harvest original."
I. Title.
PS3625.U15T48    2006
813'.6—dc22    2006004786
ISBN-13: 978-0-15-603081-6    ISBN-10: 0-15-603081-0

Text set in Mrs. Eaves Roman
Designed by Scott Piehl

Printed in the United States of America

First edition
A B C D E F G H I J K

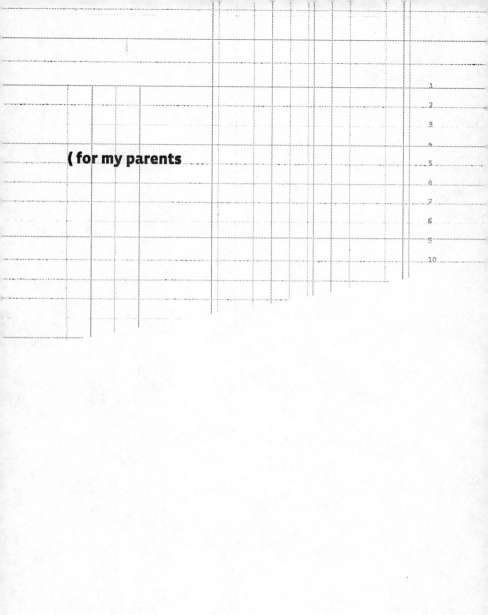

( for my parents

# ( Contents

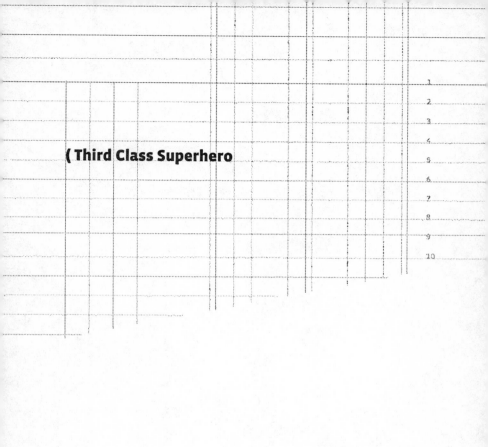

( Third Class Superhero

## ( Third Class Superhero

Got the letter today and guess what: still not a superhero.

*Dear Applicant,* not a good sign, *the number of qualified candidates this year blah blah far exceeded the number of available blah.*

I scan the list of people who did make it. A lot of them graduated with me. It's the usual assortment of the strong and beautiful. About half are fireball shooters. A few are ice makers. Half a dozen telepath/empaths. A couple of brutes, a shape-shifter, a few big brains.

One thing they all have in common is that every single one of them can fly.

I can't fly. I can't do much. On the other hand, it's not like I'm asking for a lot. I don't need to be an all-star. I just want a suit and a cape, steady work, a paycheck that covers groceries. Decent health insurance. But I'll have to wait another year.

At least I have my good-guy card. For now.

2) Charles Yu

*

Every morning, when I open my eyes, I think the same
four thoughts:

1)  I am not a superhero.
2)  I have to go to work.
3)  If I didn't have to work, I could be a superhero.
4)  If I were a superhero, I wouldn't have to work.

I was temping for a while to keep my afternoons free in
case I got calls for tryouts, but those dried up and I
needed to get a regular job for dental and vision. Now
I'm a records clerk for a big midtown law firm. I like it
because I don't have to talk to anyone or explain myself
if I'm missing for a few hours. I just say I was lost in the
stacks. People at work don't know I'm moonlighting.
They think I'm an actor.

*

Part of the problem is my name. Moisture Man. Doesn't
exactly strike fear into the hearts of the wicked.

For a few months last year, I tried to get people to call
me Atmosphero. A few people did it to be nice, but
it didn't stick—I think the problem was too many syllables. Shortening it to Atmos doesn't work either, because there's a physicist up in Seattle named Atomos
who solves science crimes with a group that calls itself
The Nucleus. The registrar says if I use too similar a

name I could be sued for infringement. She suggested the name 'Sphero, but that's just plain wrong. Makes me sound like a force-field guy, and, anyway, -o endings are usually for villains.

So I'm stuck with Moisture Man.

A couple of years ago I listed myself in the phone book, which was a mistake, because you can imagine the crank calls I get.

*

My power, if you can call it that, and I don't think you can, is that I am able to take about two gallons of water from the moisture in the air and shoot it in a stream or a gentle mist. Or a ball. Which is useful for water-balloon fights, but not all that helpful when trying to stop Carnage and Mayhem from robbing a bank.

For years I was on a self-improvement kick. I read all the books and listened to tapes. I ordered everything there was to order by mail. Studied physics, how the big brains can change gravitational constants. I read history, I learned theory, the balance of good and evil, stuff like that. Still doesn't change the fact that I'm minor. Not even minor. A sideshow. A human water fountain.

I did some time in therapy. Turns out, I have a self-destructive impulse and slight megalomania. I didn't need to pay for sixty hours of analysis to find that out. I still go to the gym, but I'm getting old and I can only do so much. I read every word of *Heroics for Dummies*. $24.99. Written by someone with an MBA. The quick bullet-point tip sheet at the back of the book tells me to "focus on my strengths" and "rely on others when it comes to my weaknesses." That's helpful.

\*

Evenings, I get home, open the junk mail, drink a warm beer. My refrigerator is unplugged and will probably stay that way forever. If I get hungry, there's a twenty-four-hour taco stand across the street. Two for a dollar and free jalapeños if you eat there. I usually get four tacos and load up on salsa.

After dinner, around ten or eleven, I go upstairs to sit with Henry. He lives in the one-room efficiency above me. He's got a futon with a thin blanket, which I set up for him years ago. I don't think he's ever changed it from the couch position. He's got one sink and a hot plate and a toilet room the size of a phone booth. Henry usually watches TV while I read the trades.

Henry is eighty-something but looks closer to a hundred and forty. His skin smells like Naugahyde and his hair pops up from his head in clumps of cotton. Up until last year, he was inhaling two packs of Reds a day, but it got too expensive. In his life Henry has poured so much booze down his throat that if he never has another drink again he will be drunk the day he dies. He's been smoked, cured, pickled, and I bet he'll outlive me by twenty years.

The way we met was this: When I moved in nine years ago, I used to hear loud banging and thumping noises from upstairs about once a week. I ignored it for a while, but one night it went on longer than usual. I went up there and knocked a few times, louder and louder. No one answered. It got quiet. I put on my costume and stood outside Henry's door for a minute.

I heard a whimper. I broke the door down—I could do that kind of thing back then. Turns out it was Henry's son, Harold, making all that noise. He had been beating the crap out of his father every Sunday night for months, an hour or ninety minutes, until he got tired. Henry had been kicked out of the house by Harold's mother thirty-five years earlier for the drinking, but instead of cleaning up his act, Henry just forgot about them and moved into this dump with his fifteen-inch television and ashtray and mini-fridge full of beer. Then Harold's mother got sick and almost died trying not to go to the doctor. Her sister paid the hospital bills and practically raised Harold, and Harold turned out all right, went to college and got married and even had a son of his own, but he was still angry at Henry.

Thing is, I believe Henry when he says he never laid a hand on anyone. I believe him, if only because Henry is the laziest person I've ever met. He only wanted to destroy himself. Did his wife deserve better? Did Harold?

Yes. Yes. Henry's not a good guy. He's getting the life he deserves and most days he seems okay with that. I forget that the majority of people don't want special powers, like Henry, who can just barely handle being normal. I don't like the guy, but I guess I have a soft spot for him because he's the only person I've ever actually protected. Even though I didn't really do anything. It was just the costume.

Since then, we've become friends. Sort of. I look in on him a little. Just a little. Not as much as I should. I'll regret it someday soon. It's true. The only kinds of people in this metropolis are failed superheroes and the lonely old men who live upstairs from them.

*

I wasn't always this way. Nine years ago, I was Young and Promising. I lived my life like I was waiting for some big event to happen. Not just a big event, but a Major Life Development. I had a lot of Capitalized Thoughts back then. I did some things I shouldn't have. I lived with about a six-month time horizon. I didn't care about the people around me. I was going places, stepping on stones, burning bridges. I had a day job, but I looked around and said to myself out loud: You people are all lifers but I'm just passing through. On my way to Big Things.

Then that first letter came and I wasn't on the list. A temporary setback. Until the next year, when I wasn't on the list again. Burnham was. Dolan was. So was Feeney. Just a bump in the road, though.

Until the next year.

And then the next.

And then four more years. I got used to it.

This year, though, I thought something was different. This year, I could feel it. I even told a couple of people. I even admitted to myself that I was nervous. This year, things would turn around.

This year hurt.

*

A few years ago, when I was doing better, I got to travel to a parallel universe, where I met a better version of myself. We talked over a beer. We got along. I tried to figure out how he saw the world. Did he have a tendency to withdraw from other people, like I do? How did he make decisions throughout the day? What mistakes had he made? I told him about the one Great Big Mistake I made a long time ago. He knew what I was talking about. Turns out, the difference between us was that one moment. I told him I kind of resented him for getting the life I didn't live. I told him what a mess I was and he just nodded. He said it would probably get worse for me.

＊

Golden Boy calls me to pretend like he hasn't heard.

"Let's go celebrate," he says.

"Celebrate what?"

"You mean . . . ? Oh, not again." Of course, he already knew. He tries to be sympathetic, but that's not one of his powers. How can he understand? He's an EM. Destined for greatness. Able to manipulate electro-magnetism the way other people chew gum. He gradu-ated two years after me and he's already got his own squad. Made Class Three on his first try, Class Two three years later. As of next January, he'll be Class One and get his own secret hideout. I'll probably never see him again.

"Next year, man." He says he'll see what he can do about getting me some work. I want to hang up but I can't af-ford to. I need his help.

When Golden Boy gets drunk, he crackles with energy. I've always wondered what it must be like to be him, to walk into a room and have everyone feel it on their skin, in their hair, their brain waves. When the earth's fields shift and warp, he says he can feel it in his limbs, in his breathing, deep inside.

＊

A couple of weeks later, I get a gig. I'm at work when I get the call. It's a mission. A real one. Golden Boy throwing me a bone. I don't know if it's out of pity or friendship. I don't know which makes me hate him more. But I'll take it. I go to my supervisor and ask for a few personal days. He says no. I tell him I have to quit on the spot. He says clean out your desk.

The turbo car picks me up in front of the law firm. Golden Boy is driving and Red Fury is sitting shotgun. I probably don't have to explain that I'm in love with her. She looks like a comic-book drawing. Her IQ is 190. On cloudy days she's a force to be reckoned with, but in direct sunlight, she is pretty much invincible. She waves at me.

I get into the backseat. Zero C is back there, reading the battle plan. He's an ice shooter. I don't know him very well, but he seems a little standoffish. Career-minded. "Try not to get in my way," he says, his breath freezing in the air.

Golden Boy tells me we're going to fight the Tricky Trio. I say that is a terrible name for a bad-guy group. He tells me to stay on task.

"We got word they are planning to steal a quantum computer from the university," he says. "It's four on three, our advantage." He said that to make me feel better, but I get the implication. It'll be a walk in the park. It doesn't matter that I'm basically useless.

We pull up and the bad guys have already done the deed. They're loading the computer into their helicopter, which is powered up and ready to take off. I take a deep breath and get ready to fight, but before I know it, Golden Boy and Red Fury are already out there, kicking ass. Zero C looks at me. "Why don't you just stay in the car?"

I wonder that myself.

But I don't. I go to take off my seat belt but it's more complicated than it looks. By the time I get out there, two of the trio are down and Golden Boy has the third trapped in an energy field. Zero C whooshes by me and creates an ice prison to hold all three until the police arrive. "We work fast in the big leagues, chief," Zero C says. "Try to keep up." I try to explain about my seat belt, but no one's listening.

❋

On the way home, I don't want them to see where I live, so I tell them to just drop me off at a bar. I go in for a drink. As I sit down, in walks Johnnie Blade. He's a gray guy—talented enough to have passed all the tests, but never bothered signing up for either side. He calls me about once a year, trying to get me to sell my good-guy card for cash. Or something better. He slides up next to me and orders whatever I'm having.

"Is it worth it?" he asks, grabbing a handful of peanuts and tossing them into his mouth. I don't answer.

Johnnie Blade grabs my wrist and locks in on me. "There are alternatives, Nathan. Quit trying to climb that ladder." He hands me his business card and teleports out. I am about to throw it away when I see the local news on the TV. The Polaris Team defeats Tricky Trio. There's Golden Boy and Red Fury and Zero C, making it look easy. Almost fun. And then they somehow got a shot of me sitting in the car, struggling with my seat belt. I put Johnnie's card in my pocket.

When I get home, I go upstairs to check on Henry. He's asleep. I startle him a bit trying to cover him with a blanket.

"How did you do?"

"We won," I say. "I kicked a little ass." Henry looks at how clean my costume is and smiles, embarrassed for me.

"Yeah, I saw you on the news. Next time, buddy. Next time."

❋

Another year of not making the cut means another year of trying to do enough freelance to keep my good-guy card, which means getting a provisional license. I sign up for the exam. The test is on a Saturday at a local high school.

Inside the exam room, sixty of us are crammed together at twenty desks. It is hot and people keep shifting around. The proctor explains the rules: three hours of multiple choice, an hour of true/false, and then ninety minutes of moral quandaries. We fill in bubbles. Name. Alias. E-mail. We describe ourselves:

What abilities do you have? Please check all that apply.

\_  Can run faster than a cheetah.
\_  Can jump more than twenty feet into the air from a standing start.
\_  Can swim faster than an adult dolphin.
\_  Can tell if a person is lying.
\_  Can intensify feelings of others.
\_  Can make others doubt themselves.
\_  Can manipulate atomic structure.
\_  Can be invisible.
\_  Can see through objects.
\_  Can see the future.
\_  Other (please explain):

There's no box to check for my power, so I write it in. Try to pretty it up a little.

*Condensation power: Can take water from the air and use it as a distraction, or to cause momentary confusion in the enemy. Also to extinguish small fires and provide refreshment for team members.*

I look around at the people in there with me. To my left is Itch-Inducer Boy. To my right is a pebble shooter.

Over by the door are Malaise Man, The Fatiguer, and The Nauseator aka Slight Discomforto. Burnouts, all of them. And they are no doubt thinking the same about me. All of us crammed into this sweatbox, each with the same thought bubble over his spandex-costumed head—*I'm the diamond in the rough, just wait, world, you've underestimated me*—each thinking he's the late bloomer, the one who is going on forty but has enormous untapped potential thus far stymied by a combination of bad luck and small-minded admissions committees.

I come to the last question and get a queasy feeling in my stomach.

Which are you applying for? Please check one.

__  Good Guy
__  Bad Guy

I check Good Guy and get out of there as fast as I can.

Two weeks later I get the provisional in the mail. I try to convince myself I don't care, but my hands are shaking as I rip open the envelope. It's a piece of gold card stock, laminated. The type is blurry and off center. What does it prove? That I know the right words to say to convince people I'm a decent guy? It's nothing, less than nothing. It's a piece of paper, a shred of the dream, but it's what I have and I want to show Henry. I run upstairs and knock. There's no answer so I invite myself in to find Henry lying on the ground.

"What are you doing, big guy?" I'm laughing at how funny he looks when I realize I am watching him have a stroke.

*

Twelve hours, three bags of chips, and two choco-dings later, the hospital waiting room is starting to feel like home. I'm trying to find a doctor to tell me if Henry is going to make it, but they keep jogging past, avoiding eye contact, which I take to be a bad sign.

A woman comes in holding her baby son. He's been nicked in the foot by a stray bullet, and the bleeding is heavier than it should be. It won't stop. The baby is barely crying, but he is bleeding all over his mother and the floor while she fills out paperwork. Where were the heroes? Something in me clicks. What the hell am I doing? What is it I want to be? A ladder climber, like Zero C? I wasn't born gifted. I'm not going to lead a squad before I'm thirty. Thirty was almost eight years ago. Even if everything I could realistically hope for goes right for me, even if the rest of my life is one long lucky streak until the day I die, where does that get me? Middle management? A teaching post? Adjunct lecturer for eight-year-olds who have nothing to learn from me, who can shoot fire and do calculus and crush my skull like a peanut?

The waiting room TV is turned to the local news. In

my world, every TV is always turned to the local news. It's like nothing else ever happens in the entire galaxy except whatever is going on in a five-mile radius to make me feel bad about myself. There's the same old story: Golden Boy and his team win again. Score one for the good guys. They interview him and I feel the chasm between us. Meanwhile, back at the hospital, I can't do anything for the one person in the world more pathetic than I am. Henry is in there maybe dying and the bleeding baby is still bleeding on the floor and I'm looking at the television thinking about why I'm not on there? About my career? A thought bubble appears above my head and there are italicized words inside it. *Don't give up. The race isn't over.* I take out my good-guy card. I realize how small it is. I feel stupid. Embarrassed for myself. For longer than I can remember, I've been pretending I don't have ambition. Hiding it from people, from myself. Pretending I'm happy where I am. I think about Henry. I think about me, about what I used to want. I don't even want anything anymore. It's a bad place to be. The race may not be over, but it's over for Moisture Man. People are starting to lap me.

I open my wallet and fish out Johnnie's card. I flip it over and over, thinking, What if? What can he get me? I go to Henry's room and look in through the glass. He's asleep. I make the call from the pay phone. While it's ringing, I keep telling myself *this is a bad idea this is a bad idea* but then he picks up.

"Talk to me," he says.

"This is a bad idea."

"Hey, Nathan, I knew you'd come around."

"Cut the shit."

"Okay, then. What can I do you for, Moisture Man?"

"I want flight?"

"Of course you do. Do you know what it's going to cost you?"

"Can you get it or not?"

"What do you think?"

It's silent for a long minute. A lifetime of guilt versus a lifetime of feeling like this. I do the moral math.

"How does this work?" I say, finally. And that's that. I feel free. I feel hollow. I want to throw up.

After I hang up, I go outside for a smoke. The nurse comes out and tells me Henry will be fine.

"He's doing well. He woke up and slurred a few syllables, but he'll be asleep for hours. Go home and get some rest."

I can't sleep in my own bed. I go upstairs to Henry's apartment to watch TV and finish the bottle of Wild Turkey he was holding when he fell over. The programming at this time of night is for people like me. People who can't believe they're watching TV at this time of night. A commercial for a technical college. A commercial for a new religion. A commercial for a multilevel marketing system guaranteed to make me up to $5,000 per week working from the comfort of my home. When the Wild Turkey's all gone, I stumble down to my apartment. I fall asleep on my couch and dream about the checks just rolling in.

*

When the phone rings too early the next morning, I don't open my eyes. I already know who it is. I already regret what I am about to do. Golden Boy is on the line. He's out of breath. Megaton dislocated his thumb and is out four to six weeks. They need a fourth. This is the real thing, he says. I want to know how many guys he called before getting to my number, but I don't ask. Can I be ready in fifteen minutes? I say I can. He says they'll pick me up in the jet.

The inside of the jet is better than I could have imagined. Every seat has two cup holders. There are free vitamins and sports drinks. My head is light from the speed and from my amorality. So this is what it feels like to be evil. Not at all what I thought. It's absolute freedom. Like stepping outside of your own body and watching it. I throw up. Zero C looks back from the copilot seat and shakes his head.

Red Fury unbuckles herself and brings me a bottle of water and some strength pills. "Here you go, Nathan." *She knows my real name* is what I'm thinking while launching into another heave. I feel her warm, photonic hand on my back, gently patting me between the shoulder blades. "It happens to everyone their first time in the jet."

I know I can't do it. I'm sure of it. With her palm pressed against my thin costume, I start to lose my resolve. Just touching her makes me a better person for a second. I want to tell her to turn the plane around. But we're already landing. Golden Boy tells us we're fighting in ten minutes. Before I can tell Red Fury what I've done, she's up and out of the jet. All three of them are out there, stretching on the mountaintop. Their muscles are all so perfect. They stretch their hamstrings. They flex and loosen their granite-like quadriceps, massage their balloon-shaped deltoids. That is what a costume is supposed to look like, I think, when it fits. That is what a superhero looks like. The reason they have better lives than I do is because they are better people. They're more this, more that, more strong, fast, smart, kind, forgiving. They're more everything. What do I have more of? What do I do better than anyone else in the world?

Red Fury is motioning for me to come join them. I can't move.

*

The battle is a rout. The good guys don't know what hit them. Apparently my card allows even a peon like me access to a lot of sensitive material. They hacked the server, got access to the battle plan. Access to the hero weakness files. Everything. I guess the good guys operate on trust. They trusted me. Halfway through, it gets so ugly I start to throw up again. I even consider fighting, but what can I do?

*

When it's all over, Golden Boy has a broken femur and a dislocated shoulder. Zero C is dead. Red Fury is basically okay except for a long, shallow cut across her shoulder. Her costume is torn. The color of her skin is impossible to describe. There's no name for it. Her gash is glowing so bright it hurts to look.

I pull together some water and cup it in my hands to wash her wound. She starts to thank me, but I stop her. I tell her what I did. She doesn't believe me at first.

"No. You wouldn't. Not you."

"Anna. Listen." My tone quiets her. I sound like a different person, admitting what I've done. I'm already a bad guy and she can hear it. "These guys are bush league. Any two of you could have taken all of them down on a given day. What happened here? Why were they so fast today? Because they *knew*. Because you were ambushed. By me. I ambushed you."

She is silent for a long time. "Why?" she finally asks, but she is twice as smart as I am and knows the answer better than I ever will. The rescue copter is getting close. I have to leave or go to jail. I climb up the stairs and into the jet. As I am flying away, I expect to see her shooting me down, but she just waves a sad, small wave.

❋

A couple of weeks later, I'm waiting in front of the 7-Eleven for Johnnie Blade. I'm on my fourth cigarette when I start to realize he might not be coming. What was I thinking, making a deal with a guy like that? Even the bad guys don't trust him.

Then he drops out of the sky and almost lands on top of me.

"You did it."

"I guess so."

"I didn't think you would. I didn't think you had the stones to do it."

I can't even look him in the eye. I wonder if I'll ever be able to look anyone in the eye again.

"Hey. Nathan. Look at me." I slowly turn my head and

stare at him with the side of my face. "You're not the devil. Get over yourself. How do you think I make a living? You think you're the first bad guy with a conscience in the history of the world? Please. Look around. Look at all these men your age wandering around in the middle of the night. No one to save, no one to save them. Think you're different? Think you're not one of 'em?"

"I don't need an after-school special from you, of all people," I say. "Do you have what I want?"

"Listen, I'm just trying to do you a favor. You weren't born a superhero. The sooner you realize it, the better."

I look straight at him. "I'll say it again. Do. You. Have. What. I. Want?"

"Tough guy, huh? Hurt a few loved ones and now you think you're Dr. Doom?" He smirks. "Okay, then. As promised." He hands me a sandwich.

"What am I supposed to do with this?"

"You eat it, big man. And then you fly."

Before I can argue, he's two hundred feet in the air.

I look at the thing. Two slices of bologna on white, a little mayo on the bread. I eat it in three bites. What choice do I have? The crosstown bus pulls up and I get on.

About two stops later I start to feel something. A tingling in my foot. My right foot. It's light at first. I'm not even sure I feel it. Then it's running up the back of my leg. Could be my sciatica. Then it's gone. Then it's there again, this time in my left foot, in the toes and heel. It's like pain. It is pain. It feels like I've been shot. I wonder if I should try to fly a little inside the bus, but people are watching. I get off twenty blocks from my stop and stand on the corner, waiting for the bus to pull away. It's late. No one's on the street. Bugs chirp. It's now or never, I guess. How do you fly? How do you try to fly? I still don't know. It's not like jumping or walking. There is a moment when you are bound by gravity, bound by rules, bound by every assumption you've ever made about yourself since the age of ten, and then the next moment you are not. In between those moments, the impossible happens. How do you fly? Not by trying. Not by doing it. Not by willpower. There's no push-off. Flying isn't an action, it's a state of being. All of a sudden, I know I can fly. One minute I have no idea how I could ever do it and the next minute I wonder how anyone could not know. I fly low the whole way home, a few inches off the ground.

From the corner of our street I can see up into Henry's window on the second floor—the dark room, the toxic blue flicker of the television.

I decide to float up to his window and surprise him. I hover for a few seconds, testing out my balance. How does it feel? Like you would expect it to feel. Better than sex. And not all that different. I want to rise, but I don't know how. Look up? Point up, with my fist, like Superman? But before I know it, I'm rising. As my head comes into view, I figure Henry is going to scream. I worry about him having a heart attack. I'm levitating outside his window. The window is open. He sees me and says hi.

"Come take a look at this," he says, pointing to his television. "This guy accidentally swallowed his own hand." He doesn't seem to notice what I'm doing.

"Henry," I say. His eyes are fixed on the screen.

"Henry, look at me. I did it. I can fly." He looks over.

"No shit."

He gets up off the futon and walks to the window. I ask him if he wants to go for a spin.

"I thought you said you didn't make it this year?"

"It's complicated," I say. "But I made it. I'm Class Three. A genuine superhero." Henry knows I'm lying before I even finish.

"I don't know what you did, Nathan. But you can still fix

it. You're not a kid anymore, but you can fix it. Don't end up like me." I tell him I don't know what he's talking about.

"You shouldn't have done it for me," he says.

Truth is, I didn't. I did it for myself. I hurt people, people who were kind to me, better people than I am. I hurt them to get something I wanted. I was the bad guy in this story. And I know it. But I wish I wasn't a bad guy. Do I get points for that? What does that make me? What kind of guy?

Henry gets on my back and we take off. Slowly, a little wobbly at first, but then smooth and fast. Flying up there with him, looking down on the alleys, the clothes drying on the clotheslines, the small concrete backyards of the city, past the city limits, to the foothills, up over the smog, I'm flying, look at me, a bad guy in a good-guy costume, no more rules. *Dear Applicant. Your help is not needed. The world is just fine without you.* That's fine with me. Fine with me that my saga isn't epic. I'm not a superhero. I'm background. I'm a good person wrapped in a mediocre soul. I want to be better. I really do. But even now in my greatest moment I know this is as good as it will ever get for me and it's not that good. I have a small heart, a dark heart, a heart filled with exactly equal amounts of good and evil, one that is weak and will take us only so far, but for now it propels us higher and higher and higher.

## ( 401(k)

1
2
3
4
5
6
7
8
9
10

Things are basically all right. I'm basically a good person. Above average, for sure. It's not always easy to know what to do. I don't know if I have a system or at least some rules or even one single rule that I follow consistently. I guess I just sort of make it up as I go along. Which is working out so far. Not so bad. I mean, considering. When I come to a place where I am forced to make a difficult choice, I draw a decision tree. If the state of affairs can be described by P, then Q. If X, then Y. If Y, then Z. And so on. Our employee handbook sets forth the official Corporate Epistemology, sponsored by Hartford Life & Mutual: the Rule of 80/20. You can get 80 percent of the way to the answer with 20 percent of the work. Good enough is good enough.

"What now?" my wife says. She says this at least once a week.

"We could get a dog."

"We have a dog."

I've got twenty-five, thirty years left. Thirty-five—maybe—maybe—if I quit with the smoking. "I don't want to outlive you," my wife says. We both know she will. It's temporary, what we've got going, and we plan accordingly.

The Realtor is showing us our dreams.

"Private, affordable, midrange," he says. I never thought I'd have midrange dreams.

We're deep in Sunday Afternoon. This neighborhood is called Luxury Car Commercial. Absolute last place I ever thought we'd be.

When we met, my wife was Pretty Girl in Import Beer Commercial. The night was young, the bar was full but not crowded, the aesthetic was clean, sleek, spare. No words were spoken. The city streets were empty and safe and artfully lit. The demos worked: 24–29 for me; she was 18–24; and we were in the same disposable-income bracket. She left before I could get her number.

The next morning, I saw her in Café/Lifestyle. She was on her cell phone and I was using my personal connectivity device. I felt Nationwide, Hopeful, Technological. *Everyone is connected,* said the Movie Star Spokeswoman, walking behind the baristas, adding depth to the mise-en-scène. *Everyone.*

I smiled at Pretty Girl over the top of my caffeinated beverage and she smiled back. The Spokeswoman regarded us with benevolent disdain. Young, thin people coming together under a common brand-self-image-identification. Love in the time of logos and franchises. A match made on Madison Avenue.

Pretty Girl and I moved in together, spent a couple of years in Mental Environment, Urban Utopia Variety.

We lived in coffee shops and wireless zones and worked flextime and walked around on the street a lot. We were part of a One Nation Calling Plan. More pedestrians per square mile than anywhere else on earth, all neatly dressed. Pressed khakis for the men. Vibrant sweater sets for the women, who were racially ambiguous and trim and nonthreateningly smooth-faced, uniformly high-cheekboned.

Before long, we longed for the suburbs, longed for Leather, Safety, and Comfort Starting at Under $32,000. The feeling, the frisson, what the philosophers call *Touring Sedan*. A primal feeling.

Which is how we got here.

"It's never too soon to start thinking about the unthinkable," the Realtor says. He pulls out a comb and runs it through his already-combed hair.

We don't need the Good Life. The Pretty Good Life would be just fine.

"Nice neighborhood," I try to convince my wife.

A quarter mile down, the street ends and turns into a winding solitary road leading into nothingness. The Realtor says that's normal for this part of Car Commercial.

"Life is about choices," the Realtor says.

"It's a little existential for us," my wife says, popping a Euphorozil.

I'm thirty-two. Or fifty-two. Or forty-two. I can't remember. Whichever one, I'm in it now. In for the duration. The long haul, the long slog. The big game. Middle age. Didn't realize until a couple of years in that it had started, and at first, I admit, it didn't seem so bad. Kind of exciting. Life-building. Dream-building. Nest-egg construction. The Grand Plan, the Master Timetable. A mortgage, thirty-year. The Big Calendar in the Sky, days like boxes, getting X-ed out one by one. Pushing the boulder up the incline. My Whole Life. The Whole Shebang. Things go fast. The decades, they get away from you. Things can get bad quicker than you think. Quicker than I thought. Mistakes count permanently. Buying things we don't want to feel closer to the things we know we can't get. The thirties and forties. The long run. The lifelong conversation. Somewhere in here we'll get incredibly lost, wander around in the desert, and get spit out on the other side of fifty-nine and a half, into the land of penalty-free-IRA-withdrawal, looking around like we just popped out of a quarter-century fun-park water slide tube, thinking, *Where am I, how did I get here, can I do it again?*

We're going to get through this, is what I tell my wife.

"Of course we are," she says. "Or, we won't." The Excluded Middle. It's times like this that I know she hates me.

We go downtown. To Antidepressants. For dinner. The sidewalks here are interrupted by lush green meadows. Butterflies are everywhere. It's bright bright green and yellow, Sad and Happy like colors, with a gritty gray undertone, as if you could wipe away the world like condensation on a windshield and see the real thing underneath. A verdigris of biochemical equilibrium.

"I make good money," I say, or ask. I'm not sure. "At least there's that."

After we got married, I got my MBA, got a job in Assurance. Reassurance, really. It's all about strategy and decisions and foresight and Regret Minimization. Planning, really. The allocation of scarce resources. Like time with grandkids. Working it out, years and dollars, so they run out at the same time.

It's hard to explain all this—at cocktail parties I just say consulting. But of course it would be a great injustice, a massive understatement, to say that the Firm does consulting.

We do consulting. We do so much more.

We envision bold new e-solutions. We help you to create a vision of the future.

We are a forward-thinking global consultancy utilizing a unique, proven value-added approach that delivers a rapid and measurable return on your IT investment. With a one-of-a-kind, ROI-focused methodology.

We do vertical integration, storage solutions, industrial automation. Supply chain logistics. Outsourcing. Insourcing. Organizational change. Knowledge flow optimization. eCRM. Supply chain management.

We do:

Marketing
PR
Proxy solicitation
Securities underwriting
M&A advisory
Reinsurance

Brand management
Risk management
Asset management
Management management

We also do copies, toilet paper rolls, toilet seat sanitary covers, urinal cakes, staplers, digital scanners, shredding, and dicing. Want to beat the S&P? Crush the S&P? We can help beat. We can help crush.

"Today is a new day," says the Corporate Gestalt on my morning commute.

The perpetually rising sun is still rising as I drive from the City Where I Actually Live, over the bridge, into the City Where I Want To Be. The dry, cool, still air smells of rich, full-bodied Ethiopian coffee beans and money. The buildings in this city are timeless, impervious. Upper Midlevel Executives stride purposefully to the beat of their own soundtracks, their eyes fixed into the near future.

Corporate headquarters is a twenty-building campus, bounded by Hope and Opportunity to the north, Change to the west and east, and Billboard County to the south. The temperature at HQ is kept at 64.3 degrees Fahrenheit.

My wife wants me to quit. She says it's killing me.

She's wrong. It's already killed me.

I look at her and I don't feel a thing.

How can I tell her that? I look at her and I know she's perfect, I know it, and I don't feel a thing. I love her, really, for real, and I don't feel a thing. The temperature inside me is kept at 64.3 degrees Fahrenheit.

I work in the Mostly Empty World. It's morning and the sun is making its way over my personal horizon. I'm global. My clients are global. The nation is asleep and the city is hitting snooze but I'm at my desk, twenty-four ounces of piping hot buzzing pure fuel in front of me.

"The possibilities are infinite," says the Corporate Weltanschauung.

I shower, get dressed for work. My wife is sitting at the kitchen table. I fumble around the pantry.

"I'll make you something," she says. "Toast."

"Did I have toast yesterday?"

"What was yesterday?" she asks.

We go weeks, years, putting off whatever it was we had started doing when we first started out doing whatever we had intended to do. When we first started out together. Young and stupid. Somewhere, our lifetime to-do list is sitting in a drawer. What is it we were going to do? We had plans, I think.

We work. We sleep.

I wake up in the middle of the night.

My wife is staring at me.

"What now?" she says.


We plan a vacation.

We want to see the Other. The travel agent sends us literature, glossies, video brochures.


We choose a package deal with Authentic Experiences™.

According to the brochure, there are five kinds of Experience: Urban, Rural, Semirural, Ethnic, and

Ethnic with Danger. Standard Endangerment is Mild or Implied, but those in the know understand they may inquire discreetly about Actual Hazard—e.g., *I've heard there might be something more?* whispered into the ear of a client services representative (along with a slip of paper, folded and pressed into the palm, on which has been written a four- or even low five-figure sum)—for which damage waiver/general release forms will have to be signed and notarized and the seriousness of the individual assessed and validated using his or her response to the questionnaire essay *What Is Wrong In The World Today?* in fifty words or less. From the brochure, we have Eric, 27, investment banker:

### What Is Wrong In The World Today

is that people are dying. Poor people. In other countries. People are dying every day, dying of death, and also disease and starvation and malnutrition. People are dying and my generation just does not care. Including me. But I want to care. I really want to. I want to care so bad.

We book a Deluxe Package. We get our shots, passports, sunscreen.

The puddle jumper lands deep in the jungle. We discover an electronic ticker flowing down the middle of the Amazon. A river of ferocious velocity. Billions of shares traded globally every second.

A man with a briefcase drops down from a tree. We've taken a vacation to get away from Car Commercial and ended up in Life Insurance/Asset Management. It's ten times worse. The big time, big budget—it's Super Bowl Worthy.

"My clients want an asset allocation strategy that takes the emotion out of their investment decisions," says the asset manager.

My wife picks up a fallen tree branch, as if to crush his skull.

"Your hopes and dreams," he says, raising an arm in defense. "A unique product tailored to fit the needs of each individual customer."

"A lot of things remain unsaid between us," I say.

"You need a management consultant," he says. "There are the obvious financial/metaphysical issues to think about, of course. And you want the whole thing to be dignified and tax-efficient."

"What whole thing?" asks my wife. She turns to me.
"What does he mean by 'whole thing'?"


We check into the hotel.

We do buffets. Midnight and breakfast. Lunch is sandwiches and iced teas on the Veranda of Opportunity. The hotel bar is open twenty-four hours a day.

The concierge informs us:

*An informed client should carefully consider all relevant factors, including, but not limited to: the general political and socioeconomic climate, both domestically and abroad, historically low/high unemployment levels, gross inequality in the criminal justice system, buoyant consumer confidence, lack of self-confidence, frenzied retail spending, sneaky retail borrowing, questionable consumer credit, evil interest rates, cutesy consumer angst, generalized anxiety disorder, pseudoreligious financial services advertising mumbo jumbo, and market volatility.*

I call down to the spa to book us husband-and-wife massages.

"You have great hands," I tell the masseuse.

The masseuse says:

*I dream of the invisible hand. I want to outsource my manufacturing. I want to protect my family from unforeseen risks. I want to incorporate a transaction vehicle to effect a tax-free 368(a) reverse triangular merger. I want to define the boundaries of tomorrow. I want to live life one choice at a time. I want to map the possible. I want to test the untestable. I want to measure the profound. I want to fathom the unfathomable. I want what I want. A wholly owned subsidiary of Global Risk International. More than life insurance, less than a mutual fund.*

We check out the pool.

The cabana boy asks me: Do I believe in an infinite power?

The poolside bartender says: Past performance is no guarantee of future results. We consider a Day Trip. The Menu of Options is truly dizzying. At the top is:

### HOW TO SPEND YOUR TIME HERE

The fine print reads:

*On a typical day, a man of your age, race, height, and moral fiber makes 4,817 distinct choices. When used in compliance with the instructions, the Basic Package guarantees a maximum of three Minor Errors and one Major Error per day. You also get three Take Backs and a midlife Do-Over.*

"When does the Authenticity start?" my wife says. "I want to have some Experiences."

We make Excursions. We pay à la carte. We explore secret islands. We take detours off the Beaten Paths. We hide in caves. We cover ourselves with mud (extra charge). We eat more buffets.

After a couple of weeks, ennui sets in. We are bored with paradise.

"Let's go home," my wife says. "I want to go home."

Home. I can picture it. We'll go back to our lives. We'll pull up the imported gravel driveway. I'll kick open the fancy imported door we bought for ourselves. It'll be Sunday Afternoon. It's always Sunday Afternoon there. Everything is perfect. Everything is fine. Ninetieth percentile. Golf is always on TV. A swirl of yearnings: a mixture of what I want, what I know I'll never have, what I am told to want, what I am afraid of, what doesn't exist. Every thirty, sixty, ninety seconds, the world completely changes. I will watch the golf, I will feel very Visit-Your-Lexus-Dealer-Today. A deep-down, in-your-gut feeling.

Our vacation is ending, our vacation is over. We pack our bags. We wave good-bye to the resort.

The captain comes on the PA. We buckle ourselves in.

Just before takeoff, I lean over and whisper to my wife.

"There's got to be more," I say.

"What?" she says. The plane is roaring.

"I said there has got to be more." I am screaming.

*Okay, buddy,* she mouths back at me, *lead the way.*

## ( The Man Who Became Himself

**HE WAS TURNING** into something unspeakable.

At the office, people avoided the issue.

*David,* they would say, *how are you? You,* they said. To be polite.

Others noticed but pretended not to. As if they weren't always staring and whispering and wondering. Assuming it could never happen to them.

David, for his part, played along, glad to make small talk. He asked about their children, looked at pictures of dogs and cats and trips to Tahoe. David moved his mouth, made the right sounds, gave people what they expected. The men talked about sports, mostly, and the women, if they could help it, didn't talk to him at all.

*

**IT HAD REALLY STARTED** a month earlier. Or not.

Whatever it was, if it was an it, it had started a month earlier.

If it was more of a lack of an it, then it had stopped about a month earlier.

Or started to stop. Or stopped starting. It had happened or not happened. Either way, something or nothing. Either way: about a month earlier.

It or not-it was not any single change. It or not-it was a lot of changes, not all at once and not connected by any pattern or nonpattern.

There was, for instance, the habit David had developed of referring to himself, daily and with increasing frequency, in the third person.

"Everyone wants to know what David's going to do," he liked to say. Which was true. Everyone did, in fact, want to know what David was going to do. It wasn't arrogance. David was, without a doubt, arrogant, but it wasn't *just* arrogance. Still, this happened often enough that even David started to notice David referring to David as David.

"I'm so sick of it," he said one night. This was near the end of the summer, during a late session at work. David was pacing in front of the whiteboard with a Magic Marker in his hand. "Everyone is always watching David."

The members of his working group nodded in sympathy. He was their boss. Also, he had large quads and round, hard anterior delts. People were somewhat afraid of him.

"You know what?" he continued. "I'll be honest. I don't know what David's going to do." He stopped and leaned over the table for emphasis. Eric from marketing was nodding like an idiot. David lowered his voice now, to drive the point home. He said, "David doesn't rush things," and then paused for effect, drawing even more vigorous nodding. "That's just not *who David is*."

There was also the matter of his detachment from the goings-on of the world. This was both local and global. He hardly watched the news anymore. Names, places, statistics—they no longer held his interest. Likewise with water rights, tree frog biodiversity, the suffering of strangers. Things that used to matter to him: populist uprisings, malnutrition, the distribution of wealth. Nothing stirred him anymore.

He had once cared.

Cared deeply and, if not deeply, then, at the very least, cared mildly. Cared in an abstract, willing-to-sign-a-petition, NPR-listener sense of caring.

Now the news just came and went, passed right through him. Now it all seemed so temporary, so specific, so far away.

Just before Labor Day, David and Patricia were having their usual breakfast. They drank a pot of black coffee with heaps of sugar added. They each ate two slices of buttered toast and then split an orange while reading their respective sections of the newspaper. David always took the business page; Patricia browsed obituaries, then cooking. They read in silence.

The phone rang. David did not look up from the stock quotes. Patricia answered.

"It's for you," she said, handing it over.

"Hello?" he said.

"David Howe?" said the woman on the other end.

And that was it.

❋

That wasn't when it happened, of course. But the day of the call was the day he remembered that, at some time in the recent past, something had happened. That, on some level, for some indefinite period of time, he had known, he had been aware, that this something had happened, although he was not sure what it was exactly.

*Two words.* That was all he had heard her say. After that, he had stopped listening. Two words: David Howe.

She had obtained David's name from a database of qualified individuals. She wanted to talk to him about an exciting new opportunity, about upside potential and risk-adjusted returns. She was good at her job and David could not get in a word for ten minutes. Finally, he hung up on her in midsentence.

He did not think about the call again until later that night, lying awake in the dark. Patricia was making small fluttering noises through her delicate nostrils. A bird outside their second-floor window was trying to mimic her nose calls. Between the chirping creature and his wife's snoring, he could not fall asleep.

*David Howe.*

That's all she had said. It was just his name. Two words. A question, nothing more.

But now he could not stop thinking about it, could not stop thinking about that moment, after she'd said it, when he'd held the phone, hands trembling, breath shallow and acidic, his vision suddenly blurry. Something in her voice, in her tone, the way she had said his name, had reached deep down and plucked something inside. That morning in the kitchen he had had a feeling, but could not quite put his finger on it and so he let it go. But now, lying in the gray middle of the night, it had come back to him. Now he could not think about anything but the call; now it was coming to him; now he remembered what had turned his fingers cold and his ears hot.

She was calling for David Howe, but she was not calling for *him*.

He remembered thinking, *She has the wrong number,* and wondering, *Why is this woman calling my house, calling my number, why is she talking to me but asking for David?* He tossed in bed for hours, got up to smoke cigarettes in the bathroom, held his head under the shower, smoked some more, the whole night back and forth, wondering how it was possible, wondering why she had called. He wondered and wondered and then, in a flash of cold sweat, he remembered. He *was* David Howe.

In the days after, he was shy, afraid of startling Patricia. He wasn't sure if she knew. If she did not, he wasn't sure he could explain, and even if he could figure out how to explain, he was not sure she would understand.

At work, he observed the different ways in which people handled what they said, how people reacted to *him*. Some people called him David, and some, as noted, preferred the euphemism "you" to refer both to David and to *him*. Mostly, though, they ignored it. They talked about what had been on television the night before. People at the office hid their fear well, which he appreciated, considering what they were looking at, all of him just out there, in the open like that, for everyone to see.

At home, it was a different story. He thought it, whatever it was, might go away before Patricia found out. He took measures to avoid her, but she made it easy. In the mornings, she woke up an hour before him, showered, drank a cup of coffee, and went to work. She was usually in bed by the time David got home. They went days with no more than a dozen words exchanged. Three, four days. A week. They barely spoke. The bills got paid, the garbage taken out to the curb. After a while, he realized she did not know. She either had not paid enough attention or he was succeeding in his efforts to conceal it, to conceal himself, the awful truth.

He thought things could go on like that indefinitely, with him going to work and pretending it had not happened and then coming home and not talking about it with Patricia. And he was not entirely sure that such a state of affairs would be wholly undesirable. At the very least, it was better than scaring her.

Then one day she came home and found David sitting on the couch, devastated. He had the TV remote in one hand, but the television was turned to a test signal. In his other hand he held a glass half full of warm bourbon.

"I don't understand how this happened," he said.

"How what happened?"

He thought she was kidding. He said nothing.

"How what happened?" she repeated.

He realized she was not kidding. Why was he hiding it

from her? Eventually, she would find out. He decided to show her. He pointed at David, at himself, at his *self*.

"This," he said.

❋

**THE BASIC FACTS** of his identity were the same as ever. His name was still David Howe. People still called him by this name when they were talking to him. Or, rather, when they were talking to David. When talking to one another, if they wanted to make reference to the person in the world associated with *him,* they said the words "David Howe" and everyone knew what they meant.

As far as he could tell, David was still the same age: forty-seven, soon to be forty-eight.

David still made the same salary, that certain amount of money transferred every two weeks out of the firm's account and into the possession of the legal entity known as David Howe. This amount was more than David rightfully deserved, and he knew it. A lot of other people knew it, too.

David still liked dogs over cats, beer over liquor, and hockey over football. David still cared about people, but only to the extent it made sense to care about them, and no further. These were the basic facts about David Howe and they did not change.

The first thing he noticed about David was that he *noticed David.*

For example, David's emotions. The basic range of David's emotions repeated itself in a fairly regular cycle: fear, desire, excitement, boredom, anger, envy. Not always in that order, but between those six feelings, most of David's waking hours were covered.

The difference was that now, when David felt something, *he* could observe it. *He* could watch the world through David's current emotional state like a slide in a projector, or as through a colored filter on a lens.

If David got angry, he could see the world through David's anger. It wasn't just the racing thoughts, the murderous impulses, or that he could feel David's face flushing bright red, David's pulse quickening. These things were not anger. It was that he knew a moment before David said something what David was going to say. He could see what anger itself looked like, how vaporous, unformed rage first cooled and condensed into fluid, volatile thought, how that liquid then crystallized around particles into individual words. He could see how David's anger was apparent to others long before David was actually angry, and long after David thought it had subsided.

Although he could watch the world as if he were every bit as angry as David, at the same time, if he wanted, he could stop. Even if David were in the middle of a rant or a tantrum or an intense fit of screaming, he could stop. Doing so did not cause any detectable wavering of David's conviction or decrease the intensity of David's anger. It was just that David's feelings were no longer *his* feelings. Feelings were optional, an activity, something he could *do*. He could choose to be angry along with David, or he could choose not to. It was as simple as that. He could do the same with happiness or sadness or jealousy. He liked the subtle variations between glee and gladness, envy and bitterness. He liked the kiddie emotions as well as the grown-up: indignation, ennui, nostalgia. David was predisposed to a postadolescent flavor of malaise in which a lot of gazing out the window was done. He liked this, too. He liked insouciance and cultivated indifference and plain old detachment. He could feel all of these, and more, just as David felt them. Still, when he looked in the mirror, he saw David. The harder he tried to concentrate, the more he saw only David. He had to remember. He *was* David.

Another change was that the past simply did not seem real anymore. Where he had gone to school, where he had worked, places he'd been. The things he had purchased, used, consumed, thrown away. All of it seemed like details in a story. But the story was not about him. David was the one who had gone to private school, who had a job at the big firm, who drove a new car. David was the one who had purchased and assembled a seven-thousand-dollar stereo system. David had been to Dublin, to Chiang Mai, to Buenos Aires. *He* had never been anywhere.

Sometimes he felt like a boy whose whole life had been spent upstairs in a small bedroom. All day long, he sat at his desk, drawing pictures and staring out the window at the backyard below, where nothing ever happened. He had been doing this for almost half a century when, one day, in walked another person who looked just like him. This person put his things down and went to another desk and began drawing his own pictures and he realized that in all those years, his whole life up to that point, he had not been living in that room alone. There had been another boy in there with him, sitting on the other side of the room, staring out an opposing window with a different view. The other boy's view was of the front yard, where everything happened. Out of that window, the other boy could watch neighbors and friends chatting, mailmen doing their jobs, kids playing, strange men driving slowly down the block and then back again. This other person went in and out of the room whenever he felt like it. He went downstairs for dinner every night. He went away to school for a while and came back grown up. This other boy, now a man, had read books, slept with women, smoked pot, married, cheated on his wife, gone to church on Easter and Christmas, and all the while *he* had never left the room. This other boy was David Howe and they had lived in that cramped space within feet of each other for their entire lives, breathing the same air, hearing the same sounds, sleeping together under the low ceiling, and they had never spoken, never even noticed each other. It was as if he was in the first person and David

Howe was in the third person and between them was an immense chasm of silence.

And even though he now knew about David, he was fairly certain David still had no idea who *he* was. He did not know if David was even capable of finding out.

The only time he thought David might have some clue about *his* existence was in David's dreams.

In one of these dreams, which was more of a nightmare, David was the captain of a lonely boat. It was a fast, sleek, powerful boat, but it was still lonely. There was no one on it except David. He stood at the helm in an immaculate captain's uniform, steering the boat across glittering blue green water, glassy and endless.

The nightmare part was that in the dream, the world was completely silent. Not one sound. Not a bird nor a breeze nor any sea life jumping into the air, not a wave slapping against the boat. The speeding prow just sliced through the ocean without resistance, without any drag or pitch, as if the boat were made of something weightless and the water could do nothing but slide off its smooth, impervious hull.

In another of his dreams, David dreamed of a man, a man who was not David. The man lived on a remote island too tiny to be on any map. The entire island was the size of a small house.

In this dream, the man could not remember ever having been off the island. No one had ever visited the island and, as far as he could tell, no one even knew he existed. The man had nothing to do except think about the boat. The man knew about the boat because once a bottle had floated to his island and inside was a picture of the captain on his boat. The man did not know what to do with it, so he kept it safe, buried in the dry sand, and, once a day, dug it out and looked at it.

In this dream, the man survived by catching small fish off his little beach. While he fished, he thought about the captain in his boat. The picture when he found it had already been faded and mostly ruined by salt water and the sun, but the man could plainly see that it was a beautiful boat. He wondered about the captain, if they would ever meet.

All day long, the man fished and slept and occasionally swam out a bit into the cove, as if this might get him just that much closer to the boat. At night, he closed his eyes and pictured the captain out there in the vast oceans of the world, gliding across the face of the calm, deep water, never stopping.

*

**AS THE WEEKS** and months passed, he grew more accustomed to being David. Not everything was for the worse. A few pleasures remained. Some were even heightened. He liked to hear music through David's ears. Rachmaninoff or Mahler. He liked David's taste in food, his preference for very hot showers. He enjoyed going to the outdoor market on Saturday mornings, especially when it rained, standing under the tarp in the middle of all the produce crates, hearing the pelting drops, the scent of ripe apples and the slightly metallic smell of rain rising off the wet pavement.

He also began to understand more than David's emotions. He began to understand belief and doubt in David, faith and knowledge, forgetting and remembering. He learned that although David felt plenty of shame and guilt, David did not feel sorry. David never felt sorry. *He* was sorry, but David never was.

In fact, being sorry was the only thing he did that David did not do. He began to suspect that the whole purpose of this, this thing that had happened, his whole purpose, apart from David's purposes, was to do just that. To *be* sorry. Not to feel sorry: If one could feel sorry, then David would have been doing it. David liked to feel everything. David was a feeling addict.

He knew David was never sorry because, in the past, David never apologized to Patricia, even when he was wrong. Now, when David raised his voice or was quick-tempered or inconsiderate with her, *he* would try to make David apologize. Most of the time, David's mouth resisted and the words came out sounding twisted and cruel or callous or insincere. But once in a while, when

David was drowsy or not paying attention, he could sneak in and say something without David interfering.

It often happened on a Saturday or Sunday afternoon when David was lying on the couch, watching television, and Patricia walked through the room, just going about her business, going about her life, not complaining much, not even complaining at what her husband had become or was becoming. He would wait until she was past him, almost out of the room, and quickly, softly, as if exhaling, he would whisper, "I'm sorry...for...all of...*this*." She would look confused, but he could tell it touched her.

Still, in time, David and Patricia drifted further apart. He began to feel that he would never be sure whether she knew or not. Sometimes he was sure she did. Sometimes he was sure she didn't. How it was possible that the woman who had lived with David for fourteen years could have trouble seeing something so obvious, seeing all that he was becoming or had become or would become, seeing *him* in all of his grotesque proportion and fleshy solidity, he did not claim to understand. Only that it made a kind of perverse sense: that the person closest to him would be least likely, or perhaps least able, to be shocked.

Throughout the autumn, many nights passed during which neither of them said a word. It seemed to get colder by the hour. Evenings they usually stayed in the same room, in the den with the heat turned up all the way. They ate dinner and then cleaned up in silence. After, David would read in the corner, an entire magazine cover to cover or, once in a while, a biography, slightly foxed, that he'd first read in college. Patricia would sit on a dusty old chair they'd bought together as newlyweds and grade her students' compositions.

Some evenings, if she finished early, she'd go to the kitchen and pour David a scotch and usually a sip of wine for herself. David would say thank you and they would sit there silently, drinking a bit, then a bit more.

On some cold, bright nights, the moon in the window, filling the room with light, they would fall asleep facing each other: David on his left side, Patricia on her right, David's hand on her hip. On these nights, he could wake up an hour or two before dawn, while David was still dreaming of boats and islands, and listen to Patricia's nose make those small fluttering noises. He would lie there inside David's body, feeling its gurgling machinery, it softly emptying and filling itself with air, just waiting until sunrise. He considered these to be good nights.

Then there were very good nights, when David had worked late or had an extra few drinks and David's body was especially tired. Being inside on those nights was like lying submerged in a bathtub filled with maple syrup. Interesting but not entirely pleasant. He could feel David's fatigue as a kind of viscosity, a massiveness. He knew David wouldn't be up for hours, and on these very good nights, he could do more than listen and lie there. On these nights, after waking, he would wait a few minutes, just to be sure, and then he would begin.

He was not entirely sure what he was doing. It was not moving. More like agitating or even resonating. It was his version of shouting, kicking, and flailing. Inside David's heavy, sleeping mass, he was small, slight, nearly weightless. But through monumental effort, he could force David's eyes open while David still slept. He strained, he agonized, he clung to every millimeter of progress. Slipping back into sleep would be defeat. More than defeat. Oblivion. He did not get these chances often and losing one was crushing. He never knew when or if he would ever get one again. He would usually have to force one eyelid open first, then the other. The second one was always easier. He had no idea how long it took. It could have been only a minute, but it felt like hours.

Once he had David's eyes open, his next task was to use David's voice box. With practice, he had gotten to the point where he could manage small whimpering noises, like a confused animal. He was not sure how David looked and sounded to Patricia. He guessed that what she saw was probably not what he intended.

What she saw was not his thrashing and flailing inside. That only registered as mild pain or discomfort or be-wilderment. What she saw was the body of her husband lying there, jaw slack, eyes watery and motionless. The first time she saw this, the first time he was able to open David's eyes and quietly stare at her in the dark, she was so terrified she fell out of bed and onto the hard floor, waking David.

But with each instance, she became less alarmed. In time, she seemed to understand that the person she was looking at was David and was not David, was her husband but was also a stranger.

They would lie there together, Patricia in her body and him in David's body and he would look at her, look right at her without any of David's knowledge or memory or guilt, he would look at her like he had never seen anything in the world before, like he did not know his own name or hers. Patricia would sit up in bed and take David's head in her lap and they would just look at each other, and for a few minutes, it did not matter what he had become, what had happened, what they could do about it. It did not matter where the boat captain was, where he was headed, where he had been. She was fine not knowing anything about him, and he was fine not knowing anything at all. He was fine just lying there inside that softly slumbering body as she stroked David's hair, saying to him, over and over again, *I know, I know, I know, I know,* while on the other side of the world, in his silent, gleaming boat, David sailed and sailed around the unending ocean.

## ( Problems for Self-Study

### 1. TIME T EQUALS ZERO

A is on a train traveling due west along the x-axis at a constant velocity of seventy kilometers per hour (70km/h). He stands at the rear of the train, looking back with some fondness at the town of (6,3), his point of departure, the location of the university and his few friends. He is carrying a suitcase (30kg) and a small bound volume (his thesis; 0.7 kg; 7 years).

Using the information given, calculate A's final position.

**2.**     Assume A is lonely. Assume A is leaving (6,3) in order to find someone who could equal his love of pure theory. A says to himself, "No one in a town like (6,3) could possibly equal my love of pure theory." Not even P, his esteemed adviser and mentor.

A suspects P is a closet empiricist, checking his theory against the world instead of the other way around.

A once barged in and caught P, hunched over his desk, with a guilty but pleasured look on his face, *approximating,* right there in his office.

## 3. RELATIVE MOTION

Across the train car, A spots B. Assume B is lovely.

(a) A immediately recognizes that B is not a physicist.

(b) Still, he calculates his approach.

(c) A wonders, Into what formula do I plug the various quantitative values of B? Could B, A wonders, though she clearly lacks formal training in mechanics, ever be taught, in some rudimentary sense, to understand the world as I do?

(d) A notes her inconsistent postulates. Her wasted assumptions. Her lovely inexactness.

(e) He decides to give her a test.

(f) A says: If a projectile is launched at a 30-degree angle to the earth, with an initial velocity of 100 m/s, how far does it travel?

(g) B notes his nervous and strange confidence, his razor-nicked chin, his tie too short by an inch, an uncombed tuft of hair. She is charmed.

(h) B humors A.

(i) B says: Well, doesn't it depend on how windy it is?

(j) Ignore the wind, says A.

(k) But how can I ignore the wind?

(l) Ignore the wind, says A.

(m) Are you saying there is no wind?

(n) A says, The wind is *negligible*. He says this with a certain pleasure. The other passengers roll their eyes.

(o) A says, It does not matter for the purposes of the problem. Besides, A says, it makes the math too hard.

(p) A looks at B's dumb, expectant, beautiful face. He feels pity for her meager understanding of physics. How can he explain to her what must be ignored: wind, elephants, cookies, air resistance. And: the morning dew, almost everything in newspapers, almost everything owing to random heat dissipation, the taste of papaya. And: the mass of the projectile, the shape of the projectile, what other people think, statistical noise, the capital of Luxembourg.

(q) A wonders: Can I be with a woman who, however lovely, does not understand how to hold all else constant? How to isolate a variable?

A thinks:

i.   she will see it my way;
ii.  she will change for me;
iii. I will educate her.

B thinks:

iv. he is lonely;
v. I can make him less so;
vi. I will change for him.

4.    A spent seven years (2,557 days, 4,191 cups of coffee) in the town of (6,3).
     He was writing his thesis (79 pages, 841 separate equations). A's thesis is on nonlinear dynamic equations.
(a) In it, he discovered a tiny truth.
(b) When he had written the last step in his proof, A smiled.
(c) A's tiny truth is about a tiny part of a tiny sliver of a tiny subset of all possible outcomes of the world.
(d) When A brought it to his adviser and mentor, the esteemed P, P smiled. A's heart leapt.
(e) P said: What it lacks in elegance, it makes up for in rigor.
(f) P also said: What a wonderful *minor* result.

5.    A and B are sliding down a frictionless inclined plane. They are accelerating toward the inevitable. Domesticity. Some marriages are driven by love, some by gravity.

## 6. THE THREE-BODY PROBLEM

Things continue to get more complicated for

A, now traveling in an elliptical path around B.
B remains fixed, giving birth to their first child.
Doctors and nurses orbit B periodically.

(a) Given the mass of A (now 80kg) and the mass
of B (now 55kg), calculate the gravitational
force between A and B using Newton's
universal gravitational formula: $Fg = \dfrac{G(mA)(mB)}{r^2}$, where G is the gravitational
constant.

(b) Imagine the situation from the stationary
perspective of B. As bodies whirl around you,
you focus on the pain, the quiet place, the
baby. Look at A, who so lovingly paces around
you, worried about your health. You wonder:
What is A thinking?

(c) Now imagine the situation from A's
perspective. You wonder: What if the child
turns out like its mother? What if the child
does not understand theory? You've spent
so many nights lying awake with B, trying to
teach her how to see the world, its governing
principles, the functions lying under it all.
Hours spent with B as she cries, frustrated,
uncomprehending.

(d) This is what is well-known in the field
of celestial dynamics as the *three-body
problem.*

(e) Put simply, this is the problem of computing
the mutual gravitational interaction of three
separate and different masses.

(f) Astronomers since the time of Kepler have known that this problem is surprisingly difficult to solve.

(g) With two bodies, the problem is trivial. With two bodies, we can simplify the universe, empty it of everything but, say, the moon and the earth, an A and a B, the sun and a speck of dust. The equations are solved analytically.

(h) Unfortunately, when we add a third body to our equations of motion, the equations become intractable. It turns out the mathematics gets very complicated, very fast.

(i) A has only recently begun to feel comfortable predicting B's path, B's behavior, her perturbations and eccentricity of orbit. And now this, he thinks. Another body.

(j) B screams with the agony of natural childbirth. She looks into A's eyes. What is he thinking, her A, her odd, impenetrable husband? Will he make a good father?

(k) A thinks generally about the concept of pain. A has a witty thought and would like to write it down.

## 7. MOMENT OF INERTIA

(a) A and B are not moving ($v_A = v_B = 0$). A is in his study, hidden in the corner. He is talking in a low voice.

(b) B, across the house, is watching television.

(c) A is talking to J, who is married to S. S is a good friend of A.

(d) J is thinner than B. S is older than A.

(e) B is listening to A. S is listening to J.

(f) Also listening: the neighborhood: Theta and Sigma, Delta and Phi.

(g) Also listening: the social circle: Phi, Chi, and Psi. Eta, Zeta, and Nu. Even Lambda has been known to listen.

(h) Others, just speculating, say that A and J would make a *good-looking couple*. A says no, thinks yes. J blushes.

(i) S exerts a force on J. A exerts a force on B. A wants to exert a force on J, and J would like it if A would exert a considerable force on her.

(j) B is walking down the hall. A can hear B. B can hear A's voice growing softer with each step she takes. A freezes in anticipation, ready to hang up the phone.

(k) B changes velocity, turns, goes into the kitchen, pretending not to hear.

(l) A does not move. B does not move. The forces cancel out. Everyone remains at rest.

## 8. PARTIAL SOLUTIONS

(a) renovate the kitchen;

(b) renovate themselves;

(c) go on safari;

(d) go to a "seminar";

(e) make large purchases of luxury durable consumer goods;

(f) make small overtures to an object of lust at work;

(g) take up golf;

(h) find a disorder and self-diagnose;

(i) get a purebred dog;

(j) get religion;

(k) landscape the backyard;

(l) have another child.

## 9. GEDANKENEXPERIMENT

(a) Imagine A is building a spaceship. He is tired of being pushed, pulled, torqued, accelerated, collided on a daily basis. Losing momentum. He is tired of his thesis failing, time and again. Every day an exception to A's Theorem. Every day he recognizes it a little less—once a shiny unused tool, a slender, immaculate volume. Now riddled with holes, supported with makeshift, untenable assumptions. A's Theorem has not so much predicted the future with success as it has recorded a history of its own exceptions.

(b) It is simplest to approach the problem of satellite motion from the point of view of energy.

(c) Every night for a year, A and B eat dinner in silence. Every night for a year, A lights a cigarette, opens a beer, goes to the garage to work on his imaginary spaceship. Sometimes, he has doubts. Sometimes, he gets frustrated, wondering if it is worth all the imaginary trouble.

(d) And then, one day, A finishes his spaceship. Even imaginary work pays off.

(e) A turns on his imaginary vehicle, listens to it roar. It makes a lot of imaginary noise. B tries to talk over it, but the engine is deafeningly loud.

(f) B shouts at A, right in front of his face. A sees B gesturing wildly. Why is she acting so crazy?

(g) The energy of a body in satellite motion is the sum of its kinetic and potential energies. It is given by the following:

$$E = K + U = \frac{1}{2}mv^2 - \frac{GmM}{r^2}$$

(h) A watches B moving frantically around the garage. A notes that B looks rather desperate, as if she is trying to stop him, trying to hold him, trying to keep him from leaving Earth.

(i) A's spaceship is heating up. It is time, he thinks. He holds the imaginary levers and calculates his trajectory. He enjoys for a minute the low frequency hum as it vibrates through his whole body. His future opens up in front of him.

(j) He is moving now. His past sealing itself
off, trailing farther and farther behind
him.

(k) The escape velocity, $v_{esc}$, of a projectile
launched from the surface of the earth is the
minimum speed with which the projectile must
launch from the surface in order to overcome
gravity and leave the vicinity of the earth
forever.

(l) His imperfect theorem, his imperfect credit,
his imperfect house, his imperfect bladder, his
imperfect hemorrhoids, his imperfect gum
disease, his imperfect career, his imperfect
penis: gone. Also gone: the history of his
interactions, his past collisions, his past. A has
finally achieved his major result. He is free
from the unceasing pull of gravitational
memory.

**10.**   A is in deep space. The solar wind is at
his back, pushing him along at a rate of
0.000000001 m/s.

At this rate, it will take the rest of his life to
travel a distance of just over eight feet. B is on a
space rock, watching A drift by glacially. Imagine
you are B.

(a) Imagine you are 20m from A. Close enough to
see his face. Close enough to know his shape.
Close enough to imagine contact.

(b) You have a rope. If you can throw it just right,
you may be able to tie yourself to A, turn his

course, affect his trajectory. You will not be able to stop him, but you may be able to make sure that wherever it is he drifts to you end up there as well.

(c) Assume you are of average strength. Assume you are of above-average compassion, patience, will, and determination.

(d) If you throw the rope and miss, what happens? If you never throw the rope, what happens?

(e) Imagine you will spend a period of eighty years within a few meters of this astronaut, a man in an insulated space suit. Imagine it is possible to drift by this man, staring at him, as he makes his way into the infinite ocean of space.

(f) You will never know any other points, other problems, the mysteries of biochemistry, the magic of literature, the pleasures of topology. You will know only physics.

(g) You will never know what it feels like inside his suit.

(h) You will never know why you are on this rock.

## 11. INITIAL CONDITIONS

A is on a train traveling due west along the x-axis at a constant velocity of seventy kilometers per hour (70 km/h). He is carrying a suitcase (30kg) and a small bound volume (his thesis; 0.7 kg; 7 years).

He stands at the rear of the train, looking back at the town of $(6,3)$: a point full of sadness, an origin of vectors, a locus of desire; a point like any other point.

## ( My Last Days As Me

The new woman is not as good as the old one. Me
doesn't like her and neither do I. On her first day, I
discover three things about the new woman:

(1) She is too short to play My Mother.
(2) She doesn't smell right.
(3) When she puts on the fat suit, she doesn't look
    like My Mother—she looks like a woman in a
    fat suit.

This causes a number of problems in the Tender
Mother-Son Interactions at the end of every episode.
For one thing, because she is so short, I have to lean
down, really almost crouch, just to put my face near
her face for the close-up.

And when I'm that close, it's hard to concentrate
because she smells so weird. If I can't concentrate,
I can't make the face for Showing Tenderness. And
if I can't make the face for Showing Tenderness,
how am I supposed to properly evoke Tinged With
Melancholy?

*

As Me, my primary job is to evoke Tinged With Melancholy, as often and as accurately as possible. For example:

## Episode 4,572,011

— **DINNER IS REALLY GOOD, MA**

**FADE IN:**

— **INT. FAMILY KITCHEN—EARLY EVENING**

**ME**
Dinner is really good, Ma.

**MA**
No. It's not.

**ME**
Yes, it is. It's really good, Ma.
These beans are really buttery.

**MA**
Are they too salty?

**ME**
No, they're not too salty.

**MA**

Too salty, huh?


**ME**

No, not at all. Not too salty.


**MA**

Too salty. I know.


**ME**

(*sudden, disproportionate anger*)

No, Ma, they are not too salty. I didn't say that.
Why would you say I said that? These beans are
buttery. These beans are perfect. These are perfect
goddamned beans. They are beautiful and they are
not too salty. Why don't you ever listen?


**MA**

I'm sorry. You're just being nice to me. They're
too salty.


**ME**

Oh my God, Ma. I just said. Oh my God. Ma!
These beans are buttery. They are not too salty.
Don't say sorry. I love these beans. I love them
so much. I'm not just saying that. I know
they're beans, I know they're just beans, and it
might seem silly, but I really love them. Please,
please. Don't say sorry. Please don't say sorry
again.

**MA**
Sorry.

**ME**
I just said don't say sorry. What are you sorry for?
What could you possibly be sorry for? I swear, if
you say sorry one more time, my head is going to
implode.

**MA**
Sorry.

**ME**
*(suddenly tinged with melancholy)*
I'm sorry. I'm sorry I yelled. Why are you sorry?
Don't say sorry.

**MA**
Sorry.

*

Just to get things straight: Me is sixteen years old. I am
twenty-two. I have been playing Me for as long as I
can remember. In that time, three boys have played My
Brother and eight women have played My Mother.

I admit, My Mother is undoubtedly the hardest role on
Family. When casting each new My Mother, they have, I
think, tried to pick a woman age-appropriate relative
to Me and My Brother. The first one I barely

remember, except that her skin was quite warm. The fifth My Mother was also very good. She taught Me to tie Me's shoes.

The most recent one, I miss her. She had started slower than any of them, during the Puberty Season. But she worked at it. She was always working at it. The technical aspects: Martyr Complex, Unbreakable Matriarch, Weight of the World. During her run, every show had a direction. Every gesture had a purpose.

Her last year was her best. That was the season Me finished high school a year early. My Father was written out of the show, the excuse being something about infidelity. The guy just wanted out of his contract. He'd been there for too long and didn't like where his character was going: the show's anchor, a stable presence, a jocular, asexual, Harmless Bearded Sitcom Dad.

That last season was the best in the history of the program. Me and My Mother averaged nearly fourteen Tender Interactions per week. Ratings for Family were at an all-time high. My Mother cried Pitifully almost every episode. She had Large Problems. It was beautiful to watch her Suffer. A true professional.

✻

This new woman, however, is not a professional. I realize that following her predecessor would be tough for anyone. I didn't expect it to go on forever. I'm realistic. If anything, I'm realistic. But this new woman. She's out of left field. She's a complete stranger. I suspect she has never played a Mother before in her life. For one thing, there is the smell. And, as I mentioned, she does not wear the fat suit very well.

Her first show is a disaster.

Family is in the middle of a six-show arc: Me gets a Love Interest, Me loses the Love Interest, Me learns a Lesson About Loss.

The scene we're shooting that day is just about the easiest scene she could ask for. Me is expecting a call from the Love Interest and goes looking for the cordless phone. Me enters My Mother's bedroom to get the phone.

## Episode 4,572,389

— **HEY, MA, HAVE YOU SEEN THE CORDLESS?**

**FADE IN:**

— **INT. MY MOTHER'S BEDROOM—EARLY MORNING**

**ME**
Hey, Ma, have you seen the cordless?

My Mother is lying there, dressed to go to the supermarket, on top of the covers.

> **MA**
> I think you left it on the kitchen counter.

> **ME**
> Thanks.

The scene should have ended there. The previous woman would have ended it there. But the new woman, she has ideas of her own.

> **MA**
> *(openly needy)*
> Can you stay in the room?

"What are you doing?" I whisper.

> **MA**
> I don't want to go to the supermarket. I don't want to go anywhere. I just want to talk to you.

None of this, of course, is in the script. I try to explain.

"There's no Interaction," I say. I vigorously mime holding a script. I try pointing to an invisible page and shaking my head.

She takes this to mean I am offering a Tender
Embrace. This is bad. She comes toward me in her
ill-fitting fat suit, tears already welling up and
smudging her makeup. Her face is a mess. I definitely
don't want to have a Tender Embrace, when it isn't in
the script, when it is early in the morning and her
breath is certain to be odd-smelling, when I barely
know this new woman.

It goes without saying a Tender Embrace in the middle
of "Have You Seen the Cordless?" is incongruous
bordering on offensive. Me has done this scene a
million times, and never has there been a Tender
Embrace. Not to mention the Openly Needy. Openly
Needy in the middle of an ordinary show. That's what
bothers me the most.

> **ME**
> (*pretending not to have noticed My Mother's open
> neediness*)
> Oh, there's the phone.

> **MA**
> (*like a little child*)
> Can you stay for just a minute?

> **ME**
> (*trying to avoid an interaction*)
> Thanks for the phone, Ma.

**MA**
*(like a little child)*
Please?

Me turns and walks out the door. My Mother weeps softly. The director yells cut.

❋

Afterward, I go out back to have a cigarette. The guy who plays My Brother is there smoking in the alley.

"Hey, man." He pulls another one from behind his ear and lights me. "Hey," I say.

This is what I know about the guy who plays My Brother: His name is Jake; he smokes a lot. In Family, he plays My Brother, who is fourteen, but Jake is actually older than me. Exactly how much, I am not sure, but he has crow's-feet and gets a five o'clock shadow by the middle of the morning. Usually we don't say much to each other.

"She'll get better," Jake says, to no one in particular. "It'll get better."
"Well, it can't get much worse."
We smoke a lot. We don't say much to each other.

❋

It gets much worse. The new woman seems determined to turn every Interaction into something it shouldn't be.

## Episode 4,572,866

— **NO ONE IS GOING TO CALL MY MOTHER ON HER FIFTY-SECOND BIRTHDAY**

**FADE IN:**

The sun is going down. Me and My Mother are alone in the house. Me is looking in the fridge. My Mother is pretending to read a magazine. The two are starting to realize no one is going to call My Mother on her fifty-second birthday.

— **INT. FAMILY KITCHEN—DUSK**

**ME**
(*comforting tone tinged with melancholy*)
Hey, Ma. Happy birthday. How about we go to dinner?

**MA**
(*not even trying to hide disappointment*)
Thank you. You don't have to do that.

**ME**
(*comforting tone tinged with melancholy*)
So, where should we go to dinner?

**MA**
*(barely concealed fear of growing old alone)*
I don't care. You choose. Italian?

**ME**
*(realizing comforting tone is not working, wondering what to say next)*
Okay. Italian sounds good.

**MA**
*(unbounded terror at realizing she is being comforted by her own child)*
Great. Let me get my coat.

**ME**
*(wondering what to say next)*
I'll start the car.

The director yells cut.

\*

I go out back to smoke. Jake is there.

"Was she awful or what?"
"I don't know, man. You know? She's not so bad."
"She's not so bad? She's not so bad? She forces her lines. She forgets her lines. She makes up her lines."
"You used to do that."
"Not like that. I didn't look like a deer in headlights.

She's turning what should be normal Melancholy into something else. Something formless and terrible. No name for it."

"What are you going to do?"

"I don't know. Get her fired, maybe."

"Man. You gotta chill. It's just a job."

Jake is very good at what he does. He's much better at Being Him than I am at Being Me, and he knows it. I suspect he thinks he's too good for Family, that he won't be here long, that it's only a matter of time. I also suspect he's just a natural, that he doesn't have to try very hard at Being Him, and sometimes, I have to admit, that makes me mad.

They don't write many Interactions for Me and My Brother. A couple of seasons ago, we had a tense Angry Brother-Brother Interaction, but not much since.

✽

On my day off, I go to the park. The air is cold and imperfect, not canned like in the studio. Ambient noise drowns out my inner monologue. I don't have to hear the soundtrack to Family piped into the building, a continuous loop of faint music. I take out my pocket-size writing tablet and a pen and place them on the bench beside me. At the top of the page is written: How to Be Me.

Five-year-olds are playing soccer nearby. More specifically, they are viciously kicking one another in the shins while a soccer ball sits unharmed in the vicinity. Once in a while one of them inadvertently kicks the ball, causing a considerable amount of confusion. But mostly they leave the ball alone.

In the mass of yellow green jerseys and purple silver jerseys, one boy is moving with more decisiveness than the others. He breaks away from the pack and kicks a low, squirting goal through the orange cones. The ball rolls to a stop a few yards from my bench. The boys look at me expectantly. I kick the ball back to them, too hard. We all watch as the black and orange orb sails over their heads and lands next to a dog, who sniffs it.

I light a cigarette and take a sip of iced coffee from my thermos. The cold liquid spreads through my chest cavity. I can feel individual rivulets moving through me. I consider asking the boys if I can join them, maybe as goalie. The parents are still eyeing me warily after my overexuberant kick. I want to tell them it was an accident, that I would like to play soccer with their kids.

I stare at the blank page.

How to Be Me

1.
2.

3.

4.

5.

6.

7.

8.

9.

10.

I don't remember why I picked the number ten, if it was optimism or just a nice, round number. Or maybe pessimism. Are there ten ways to Be Me? Why not nine? Why not a thousand? I think about calling my predecessor, but then I remember I don't even know where he lives.

The soccer game ends. Hugs and oranges all around. There is talk of pizza and arcade tokens. A round of yays and cheers goes up as boys pile into cars and utility vehicles and vans in twos and threes.

＊

The next day we have a short scene. It has been raining since before dawn. Me and My Mother have been moving from room to room aimlessly all morning. The house is completely silent. After lunch in front of the television, My Mother asks Me to teach her how to use e-mail.

# Episode 4,572,513

**—I AM A VERY NICE PERSON**

**— INT. THE COMPUTER ROOM—EARLY AFTERNOON**

My Mother is sitting in front of the computer, hands resting on the keyboard.

> **ME**
> Okay, Ma. Let's try to send an e-mail. Who do you want to send it to?

Silence as Me realizes My Mother has no friends.

> **MA**
> *(pretending not to realize the same thing)*
> Myself.

> **ME**
> Okay.

> **MA**
> What should I write?

> **ME**
> Something, anything. It's just a test.

She sits motionless with her hands on the keyboard.

**ME**
Ma, it's just a test message. Write the first thing
that comes to mind.

She types: I am a very nice person.

She's supposed to just type gibberish, whatever,
anything at all. Not something pitiful and honest and
childlike. Not something that makes no sense except
for loneliness and hunger for love. And who is she
trying to convince?

**ME**
(*trying to avoid a Tender Interaction*)
That's good, Ma. Now click Send. See that little
tiny envelope? That's your message that you just
sent. Click on that.

She opens the message and reads it aloud.

**MA**
I am a very nice person.

The director yells cut.

＊

I've finally figured it out.

"She's a faker," I say to Jake. But Jake's half drunk and
not really listening. It's ten in the morning.

"She can't do Tedium. She sucks at Anxiety. She sucks at Quiet Desperation." I pick up a dirt clod and hurl it against the alley wall. It explodes softly into smaller clods.

"Not everyone's, you know, a Serious Actor like you," Jake says. "You know?" He hiccups.

"What does that mean? What is that supposed to mean?"

He takes a long drag off his cigarette and looks away.

"Hey," I say, "what is that supposed to mean? Answer me."

"Look, man. I like you and I like you as Me. But, all I'm saying is, you know? I mean, just relax? With your, what do you call it?"

"Creative research."

"Yeah. Always trying to, I don't know, be whatever."

"Me. Be a better Me. What's wrong with that?"

I realize he does not feel the same way I do about our smoke breaks. Suddenly I feel very silly for thinking I knew this guy who plays My Brother, for thinking he took anything seriously.

We smoke and don't say anything for a while.

"She's not Poignant," I say, finally breaking the silence.

"What's Poignant? There is no Poignant."

"She's not genuine. She's not real."

"Real? What's real? Just read the lines and stand on your mark and try not to miss any cues."

\*

That night I proceed to get drunk on the set. I wake up slumped over the kitchen table. I have a hangover that feels like someone let a cat loose inside my face. Half-empty beer cans are all over. Next to me is an ashtray full of Parliaments smoked down to the filters. I hear birds outside chirping like winged demons. I want to be one of them. Or, alternatively, I want to clip their wings and then shoot them all.

Down the hall, I see the new woman walking toward her dressing room. She stops in front of the door and looks at me.

"Hello," I say.

It might be the alcohol or the difficulty I am having in staying vertical that focuses my mind. But I realize I am looking at her for the first time. Really looking at

her. Her face is scrubbed clean and she is wearing a
T-shirt I wore two seasons ago. It goes down to her
knees and hangs off her narrow shoulders like a cape.
She wears sweatpants from Wardrobe. Probably My
Brother's. She is so small and so mammalian—the
texture of her skin, the damaged coarseness of what
must have once been beautiful hair.

I ask her what she is doing here in the middle of the
night.

"I can't sleep," she says. "So I came here to work. I
want to do a good job for this Family."

I want to say, How can you do this? What do you
think you are doing? You can't state the premise.
You can't just say that you are Sad, that you want to be
Comforted. There are rules, and there are times and
places and manners for Showing Tenderness. I want to
say, don't say it. It's better if you don't say it. But she is
so small and she is a stranger and all I can manage to
mumble is "great job," not knowing what to do but lie.

"Thanks," she says, looking at me quickly before
slipping into her room.

❋

A week later, I show up on the set and the new Me is
already standing there, talking to the writers. I guess I

should have seen it coming. What with the new woman and her way of doing things and also the discovery of Jake and who he is and how little he cares about playing My Brother. I should have seen the direction things were going.

People in the crew look at me like they have never seen me before—makeup, grips, guys I've known for years. Just like that, I am nothing to them, now that I am no longer Me. I wander around, fingering the cheese cubes on the snack table and smoking cigarettes, trying not to watch Me, but watching Me anyway. He's about the same height, maybe a hair taller, and has a sunken look to him. They're shooting "Dinner Is Great, Ma." I see Jake standing in the corner. He waves and comes over.

"Sorry you had to find out like this, man."
"When did you know?"
"I didn't."

"I don't believe you." Film is rolling. Someone shushes us. We watch for a while. Then I see that Jake has been replaced, too. Some college guy, full in the shoulders, with the cuffs of his Oxford button-down rolled over his meaty forearms. He looks like he's straight from a catalog.

"This guy sucks at Tinged With Melancholy," I say, out of jealousy. And it's true.

"Yeah."

"I mean, he really sucks at it."

"Yeah. He sucks."

"What?"

"What?"

"You're thinking something."

"No, I'm not," he protests. I give him a look.

"It's just that, well, I mean, don't get me wrong, you're good at it, you were very good at it and when it was on it was on."

"But."

"But, well, why did it always have to be Tinged With Melancholy?"

Then I see his point. A huge pit opens up in my stomach and my cheeks get hot and the tops of my ears, too.

The way the new Me says his lines, he hits Comfort right on the head. His pronunciation of "buttery," his rich, liquid sounding of the word "beans." He is so good everyone forgets they are watching a show. It gets very quiet. Crew guys stop talking.

Already my fumbling attempts embarrass me because I can see My Mother is Happy. Already I wonder if she, if anyone watching, will ever miss my flawed puny experiments, my willingness to be Melancholy, my amateur efforts to properly Love My Mother. My search for happiness through Sadness.

The new Me can't do Melancholy, but he can do pretty much everything else. He can do Tedium. He can do Ironic. He can even do Secret Joy. The advanced stuff. But the thing is, I get the sense he doesn't even know the names. He doesn't think: Now Me should tilt his head this way and furrow his brow just so to Self-Deprecate, to Commiserate. He's past that. Where I played wobbly individual notes, he plays chords. Huge, booming, double chords, eight, nine, ten notes struck simultaneously, with differing amounts of force, all of it coming out together.

I wonder, why did I always have to tinge everything with Melancholy? Why did I think it was all about Interactions? Why did I have to capitalize every Emotion? Why didn't anyone explain that all I had to do was lean down, crouch down, and forget the script and ignore the weird smell coming from her and say, to My Mother and to the strange woman in the fat suit: I'm Sorry uppercase and I'm sorry lowercase and I Love You and I love you and I'm here, Your Son, a stranger, a guy trying to play him. We're all right here.

## ( Two-Player Infinitely Iterated Simultaneous Semi-Cooperative Game with Spite and Reputation

**1**

The highest score of all time was recorded on July 24, 2016.

**2**

On that date, Wally Kushner, age seven, of Eureka, CA, achieved a point total of 1,356,888, including all bonuses.

**3**

Using a modified Stupps-Kinsky approach (1973), Wally conducted a single-session game lasting more than nine thousand rounds. In total, he played for eleven days, six hours, twenty-four minutes, and three seconds.

**4**

Wally's mother kept time. She also fed Wally and wiped down his face and neck with a damp washcloth. She did this twice a day, once in the morning and once in the evening.

At the conclusion of the game, Wally, then seated cross-legged on the floor of his bedroom, looked up at his mother. He asked her, "Are you proud of me?" Wally's mother was very proud.

**5**

The game begins when a player walks into a room and announces a statement. The statement can be a truth or a falsehood. If another player is in the vicinity and hears the announcement and if such other player has his setting switched on to Accept Truths, then the program will engage. The subroutines will be loaded. This is the beginning of a game and this is how a game always begins.

**6**

During his marathon effort, Wally consumed forty-three bologna-and-cheese sandwiches, seven and a half gallons of orange juice, and one hundred ninety-one Oreos. His average pulse during the game was a placid sixty-four beats per minute. Doctors monitoring Wally noted his almost total lack of perspiration.

**7**

The program run-time summary from Wally's record session reported that Player I, controlled by Wally, made exactly nine thousand and forty statements. Of these, five thousand were statements about the world, four thousand were statements about other players, thirty were statements about himself, ten were statements about all of the above.

Seven thousand five hundred statements Wally made were true, one thousand five hundred were false, sixty statements were both true and false, ten statements were neither true nor false, one statement was false and beautiful, one statement was neither true nor false nor beautiful, but it was funny and sad and sweet and, on top of it all, grammatically correct.

**8**

The basic tool in the game is the eye-looking vector. Each player has one. The eye-looking vector starts from the center of the player's head and extends forward, parallel to the sagittal plane and orthogonally to the coronal plane of the player's body. Players can point their eye-looking vectors in a ninety-degree peripheral field of vision from their line of forward orientation.

**9**

Another important tool in the game is the vector-accepting eye. A vector-accepting eye is the same as an eye-looking vector. They are two names for the same thing, but they are described with different terms, depending on the current polarization of the players.

**10**

A general rule of thumb is this: When a player is announcing the truth, he looks with an eye-looking vector. When a player is accepting the truth, he accepts with a vector-accepting eye.

**11**

The average eye-looking vector is three yards long. Within the range of the eye-looking vector, a player can absorb data and make true statements about the world. The length and spatial orientation of the eye-looking vector determine the statements about the world that can be made. The longer the eye-looking vector, the more statements a player can make about the world. These might be true or false, beautiful or not beautiful, but these are the only statements that can be made.

Note, however, that even a very long eye-looking vector cannot help a player make statements about other players. More about this later.

**12**

Wally began his game by choosing Player 1.

**13**

Each player must assume certain things about himself.

**14**

Wally chose the Husband-Wife module.

He assumed the following:

"I am thirty-seven years old."
"I make more than I deserve."
"I have a beautiful wife. I know this because everyone tells me so."
"As far as I can tell, I have no attachments to anyone or anything in the entire world."

**15**

Other modules include Brother-Brother, Father-Son, and Total Strangers.

**16**

Mirrors are an interesting feature of the game. A mirror will turn a vector in a different direction. Mirrors can confuse the difference between eye-looking vectors and vector-accepting eyes. Another feature is the black box. Not much is known about the black box.

**17**

The Sorry Feature has been updated for more
realistic game play, especially between lovers or
strangers.

**18**

Another updated feature of the game is
Common Knowledge. Common Knowledge is
activated in the following situation. If Player 1
walks into a room and makes a true statement
and Player 2 is within range and hears the
truth of the statement, Common Knowledge
may be attained. What has to happen is that
Player 1 must utter the true statement while
pointing his eye-looking vector in the
direction of Player 2's vector-accepting
eye. Player 2 hears the truth and knows it.
Because Player 1 is eye-looking, Player 1 knows
that Player 2 knows the truth. Because Player 2
is eye-looking, Player 2 knows that Player 1
knows that Player 2 knows the truth. Likewise,
Player 1 knows that Player 2 knows that Player 1
knows that Player 2 knows the truth. An
infinite hierarchy of knowledge is created. This
can be depicted as a spiral between the players,
each one knowing an infinite number of truths
about the other.

**19**

Wally writes:

*A lot of people spend too much time deciding between Player 1 versus Player 2. This is the first mistake, in my estimation. Everyone I talk to wants to know how I got my high score, but when I tell them, they refuse to believe. Most readers of your magazine will not believe it either, I'm afraid, but I'll say it again anyway, in case anyone out there is open-minded.*

**20**

Wally also notes:

*Sorry is not what it seems to be. This is the main thing that makes me different from your average player.*

*Your average weekend player thinks Sorry is used as a defensive measure, to block eye-looking vectors.*

*The professional uses Sorry as a neutral move.*

**21**

Wally concludes:

*When the amateur says Sorry, he means: I wish that had not happened, but the world is what the world is.*

*When the player of strength says Sorry, he means: That happened.*

❋

Neat Trick: Also, thanks to Wayne Garza of Grand Rapids, MI, for the Trick of the Month.

Wayne writes:

*Common Knowledge works in the mirror, too. To use it, go into Player 1's house. This is at the very beginning of the game. The program will place you in the town square. Walk two units south and one unit west. Find the white house with a blue roof. Go in. (The door will be locked. The key is under the mat.)*

Our staffers have verified that Wayne's tip works. To try it for yourself, follow these directions:

A. From the entrance, go down the main hall to the second door on the right. This is the guest bathroom. Turn on the shower. Make sure the water is very hot. Close the door and let the bathroom fill with steam.

B. When the mirror is cloudy and opaque with the condensation from water vapor, stand in front of the mirror, about a foot to eighteen inches away. This is the optimal length for all eye-looking vectors. At this length, an eye-looking vector has unique properties. Use your hand to wipe off a small area—maybe six inches by three inches—from the glass so that the mirror can reflect your eye-looking vector. Now look at yourself. Keep looking. Do not look away. Stand still. Do not look away. The game will ask you over and over again if you want to look away. Resist the temptation. Note what is happening. Your eye-looking vector will begin bouncing off the mirror and into your reflection's vector-accepting eye, and then back out again. The vector will keep bouncing, back and forth, into the mirror and then out, into your own head, and back.

C. After a while, small windows will pop up and the game will ask you over and over again: Are you sure Are you sure Are you sure Are you sure? Click away all of these little boxes. New windows will spring forth, asking if you want to terminate the subroutine. The game will assume there has been some kind of error. Keep clicking these closed, too. Stand still and whatever you do, do not look away.

D. If you wait long enough, the game will give up and override the defaults. It will recognize your reflection in the mirror as a different player, Player 2. Now you are Player 1 and your reflection is Player 2.

Now, say you are sorry. Say a true thing. You will know it and you will know you know it and you will know you know you know you know you know you know you know you know you know it. You will know an infinite number of things about yourself, an infinite regress, telescoping up to a vanishing point, a hierarchy of statements, longer and longer, more and more abstract, receding into the distance, farther and farther from the world, none of them beautiful, all of them true.

## ( Realism

**MY MOTHER IS READING A BOOK** called *Realism*.

It is a collection of stories, arranged like a museum. She bought it for herself. For her birthday. She is hoping it will help her understand her life better.

"Why do they call it realism?" she asks.

"It's not really realism," I explain. "Realism is just another way of choosing facts about the world."

"That's confusing," she says.

I say to her: You take a person and list some of her physical attributes. Make them seem significant.

I say: You accumulate details, where that person lives, what she likes to eat, what she sees from her kitchen window every morning.

I say: You make time flow evenly, in a straight line, one instant to the next. Events occur in some logical order.

Effects follow causes. What has already happened and what has not yet happened are divided by a thing called the present moment. There is a thing called memory. That's realism, I say.

My mother will not admit it, but she bought the book because she felt she needed to read it before she couldn't read anymore. Before it was too late.

My mother is going to die.

My mother is going to die, my mother is dying, my mother has already died.

All of this happens in one night. The night she dies. All of this happens in one frozen frame in the flight path of Xeno's Arrow. In the luminiferous aether between Point A and Point B. Between two arbitrarily close points on the infinitely dense real number line.

Everything that will ever happen has already happened. Xeno's Arrow doesn't really ever move.

What is a story in this kind of universe? What is character, what is plot?

*

"Listen," my mother says. "I think you will like this."

She opens the book and begins to read:

And then in one moment, I understood what he meant, I understood everything he had ever meant, and had not meant, and could have possibly meant in all possible and impossible worlds. I felt melancholy, I felt joy, I felt dread, I felt a sadness so deep it cannot be described in words. I felt emotions that have not been given names, I felt emotions that have been given the wrong names, I saw what it meant to feel and I saw that it was all the same feeling and I felt big feelings, the old feelings, the ones before language, before the mind had language, before the mind had learned to tell a fake story called consciousness and developed anxiety when it invented time, and danger, and risk, and probability, and the future. I felt what the caveman felt, staring up at the young sun, before division, before naming, before fear and awe and desire had been created. I felt that first unified feeling of what it is to be alive, to be human, to know and therefore not know. And I felt small feelings, too, the most trivial, the most subtle feelings others would not distinguish between, I felt all of them, a million kinds of sadness, a trillion, every variety, every infinitesimal gradation, I felt them all at once and one at a time, in a single moment. I stepped out from my front door and into the daylight and took a long sip of my foamy, frothy cappuccino. It was a new day.

This is from her favorite story in the book.

The title of the story is *Once More, with Feeling.*

It is a story about a sudden moment, an invisibly thin sliver of the life of the mind of a young man trying to understand things he will never quite grasp.

My mother wants me to make our lives into this kind of story. A realistic story. She thinks I can do it.

"I want to feel like that young man in the story," she says. "I want to feel small feelings."

This is why she bought the book. To teach herself the names for her nameless life. To learn that people have cataloged her anonymity. She has been mythologized.

My mother has discovered her interior life. It has always been there, a roiling primordial ocean, a vast and deep and fluid planet inside her, a world of limbic forces and unformed, half-formed, preverbal objects floating in the surface waters of her consciousness, in the benthic depths of her unconscious—massive, silent, underwater objects bumping her occasionally from within. This ocean is something she never thought to talk about, as if it were an unspeakably private derangement, something others would never understand.

And now she is like the cartoon coyote, suspended in midair, who is reading a book about gravity and after learning what gravity is, begins to fall to the earth. Now that my mother knows that all of these feelings have names, that there are empty containers for her to fill, to pour her amorphous, unrefined emotion into, she must do it. She must learn the names for the things that have always been there inside her.

*

She reads. Thirty years go by, forward and backward and forward again. Time stops and starts and stops again.

"This book, it kind of makes me seem pathetic," she says. "I never realized I was so ordinary."

I tell her that's the point. I tell her I am ordinary, too.

"Most people are," I say. "That's what it means to be ordinary."

She tells me that when I was born, she thought I was going to be a great man.

"That's what your name means. It means Marching Toward Greatness."

My mother's life up to this point has been a record of small insults, neither tragic nor inconsequential. She lives alone. I am her only visitor. She has taken to watching the Lifespan Network, a twenty-four-hour continuous feed of made-for-TV movies, star vehicles driven by B-list actresses. B minus. The movies are XXX poignant, long stretches of aimlessness punctuated by brief interludes of emotional gratification. Pornography for the heart.

"I want to go through an experience. I want to have an epiphany," she says.

I tell her there is no such thing. I tell her those are made-up features of realism. Illusory. Like time, like meaning.

We work, we sleep, I live my own life. She lives hers. We used to see each other once a week, then it was twice a month. Now it is once a month. But we are always talking. We can talk through walls. We can talk across the city. We can talk from different countries, different planets. The universe is one big living room, all of space and all of time from the big bang to right now has been one long conversation between the two of us.

"I want to try out all of these new emotions I learned about," she says. "I want to feel weltschmerz. I want to feel malaise, six kinds of it. I want to feel ennui.

"What is ennui?"

I tell her ennui is an emotion for rich people. It is like boredom, but more refined, like high-thread-count bed-sheets.

My mother is getting impatient.

"So far, you aren't doing a very good job of writing our story," she says. "This is going nowhere."

She becomes voracious. She needs more. More, more, more. Stories, stories, stories. Everything is a story to her now. Everything.

✽

"Why *Realism*?" I ask her. "Why does this matter to you?"

"It doesn't. That's the point. You have to make it matter."

I am trying to make a story out of the raw material of our lives. I can't connect the pieces. I have to try to stitch them together with fragile threads that break and fall apart. Sometimes just looking at them too hard, just thinking, makes everything fall apart. I need to do this before she dies. I need it to matter. How do I do that? How do I keep it from just trailing off?

My mother tells me I have already covered all of this.

She says I need a driving force. Instead, I am going in circles.

"We have a beginning and an ending already. It's the middle that is difficult," she says. "We are missing a middle."

I know we are. But if she wants it to be real, to be real-ist, to make sense, then there is only so much I can do.

✽

From *Realism,* chapter 30, page 2,157:

She reads: "Skilled practitioners often include details to increase the believability of the narrative. Note, however, that this use of particulars detracts from the universality of the story."

My mother asks me, What is universal? What does this mean?

I tell her something is universal if all people can understand it. Truths about the human heart are universal. At this, my mother laughs, as if I have told a good joke.

"*Realism* has more nouns, more adjectives. Where are the thousands of varieties of flowers? Where are the descriptions and terms for architectural features? Describe my nose. Describe the smell of the tree in our backyard. Enough of your abstractions."

She says I keep coming back to the same few words. Like I am stuck. Over and over again. She says I am obsessed with time, space, death, consciousness, memory, risk, the world, the universe. She asks me, Is that all you know? Is that all there is?

I can't make this about us, I say. Your life is not what you did, what you said or wore or ate or drank or noticed out of the corner of your eye. I have to leave out the details, I have to find the essence, search for the missing middle. I have to keep this general. I have to find the secret at the center of our story. Then I will be able to tell it. Then I can fix the beginning, sharpen the ending. Then I can fill in the exposition.

"We are running out of time," my mother says. "I'm going to die any minute now."

*

She needs me to make it matter, to make some sense of things before she dies. I have said this all before. After she dies it will be no good to her. She can always come back to her life, we can always start this whole thing over again, but then we will be back at this point. This point right here. I have to make it make sense during her life, inside of her life, within it. I can't reach out, go above it, tell a larger story, a story-within-a-story. I can't cheat. Not if she wants realism.

But what if that's the whole point? What if it is impossible to make it matter before she dies? What if that's what death is? The truncation. The explanation. The symbol key to the fumbling, inexact allegory of this condition.

We are nearing the end, and still there is no urgency. No order to anything. I keep repeating myself. My mother knows it. We are drifting.

"You don't have to make it up yourself," she says. "We are almost out of time. Just make it work."

"All stories have already been told," I say.
"Then tell me someone else's story."

I tell her the story about a man who wakes up one morning to find himself transformed into an enormous insect. He thinks but he cannot express himself. He is isolated, alienated, a consciousness in a grotesque form.

That's funny, she says. When I was a little girl, my uncle, your great-uncle, would tell me a similar story.

This was the story:

> One morning, an insect wakes up to discover he
> has been transformed into a six-foot man.
>
> The man gets out of bed and stands on two legs for
> the first time in his life.
>
> He bathes himself free of slime, puts on a starched
> shirt and pressed suit, drinks a cup of coffee, kisses
> his human wife, and goes to work.
>
> At work, he sits in his cubicle all day. Then he goes
> home, goes to sleep, gets up, and does it all again
> the next day. His boss likes him so much he
> promotes him and then promotes him again.
>
> The man lives out the rest of his life like this,
> never a thought in his head, and no one ever
> knows that inside he is an insect, shrieking and

shrieking in insect terror inside his huge, empty brain. No one ever knows that he is nothing but a big bug, a dumb, senseless cluster of impulse and sensation trapped in the strangest of all horrors: human consciousness.

*

My mother tells me this story. And then she dies.

Time stops. And then time starts up again. I am alone.

*

Time loops back.

My mother is alive. We are in the kitchen again. She is reading a book called *Realism*.

"I'm going to die soon," she says. "So we have to work fast."

*

She dies again. She keeps dying and coming back. I tell her I am trying my best.

"What if you can't do it?" she says. "What will happen to us?"

I tell her that not all stories have endings.

Yes, they do. Yes, yes, yes, they do, she insists. They end where they end, where that place is, wherever they have taken you.

"We can't fail," she says. "I want to feel everything. I want to feel every emotion ever felt. I want to learn something. I want to be trapped in a moment, forever, at the end of my life, in amber, in a frozen instant of genius."

We will fail, though. We already know we have. She has lived this moment a thousand times. A hundred thousand. Our entire lives together are nothing more than this moment. The two of us, a son and mother, trying to have a lifelong conversation, trying to make some sense of their anonymity, themselves.

All stories are failed stories, I say. All real stories are stories that failed at being the ideal story.

I try to make things happen. I try to drive us toward something, anything. I have no great secret to tell her, nothing that will tie it all together. I'm not smart enough to do it. Some stories have no beginning or end or middle. Some stories do not exist. There are some places you can't get to.

I give up.

"I can't do it," I say. "I can't make this into a story."

## ( Florence

A message comes through from the boss.

*How is she?*
I look over at Florence's vital readings.
The machine blips.
I type: *Normal. The blips are blipping.*

Four years go by.
A message comes through from the boss.

*How about radius? Stable? Or getting bigger?*
Florence swims in a circular path around the lake.
I check the display.
I type: *Radius is stable. 41.08 kilometers.*
I hit Send. Four years go by.
A message comes through from the boss.
*Velocity?*
I check the velocimeter. *8.2 km/h.*
Four years go by.
*Good,* says the boss. *Good.*
*Thanks,* I say. Four years go by.
More questions from the boss:

*Skin tone?*
*Discoloration?*
*Cartilage loss, fin damage, decreased mass?*

Blip. Blip blip. I report:
*No change.*
*No change.*
*No change, no change, no change.*

Four years go by.

*Good. Anything else?*
*No.*
Four years go by.
*Good,* he says. *How's life on your rock?* He doesn't make
small talk often.
*Same old,* I say. *Can't really complain. Yours?* Four years go by.
*You know. Same.*
*Yeah, I know.* Four years go by.
A world explodes in a nearby system.
*Is Tina coming soon?*
*In a bit,* I say. Sixteen hundred years.
Four years go by.

*Say hi for me,* he says.

*Okay.* Four years go by. Four years, four years, four years.

*You okay with money?* I say I am. I say I live at the edge of
the universe. Where am I going to spend it? Four years
go by. *Why?* I ask him. Four years go by. *No reason.* Four

years. Four years then four more and then four more and just like that seven or eight hundred years can go by and we haven't said a thing.

*

The last time I saw Tina, I asked her to stay on the planet with me. She said it was too cold for her. I said I'd reconfigure the atmosphere, trap some heat, warm up the place. She said she couldn't imagine quitting her job. I said, You deliver cubes of frozen fish for a living. She said she needed the money. I asked her, What are you saving for? The galaxy is in a recession. There's nothing left to buy. I said, The nearest grocery store is two hundred and eighty thousand light-years away and the only things it has worth saving for are the long-stalked sentient mushrooms of Nlakdaviar. She said she had a weakness for those mushrooms. I wanted to tell her I had an entire mountain hollowed out and full of the fungus, cut from the base in early autumn, so the tendrils were white and springy and full of moisture. But I didn't. Instead, I said nothing. It's too cold for me, she said again. She waited for me to say something. Fifteen seconds went by. I wanted more than anything to make my mouth say something. I searched every word in every language I knew, I picked up each one and discarded it—not the right word, not what I mean, not going to work, not enough to make her stay. I did this in fifteen seconds. She looked at me. Hopeful? Annoyed. I said nothing. Another fifteen seconds went by. I let them go right by. Tina flew away. Four years went by. Thirteen thousand two hundred and fifty-one years went by.

\*

A message comes through from the boss.

*What's new?* More small talk. Something's not right.

It's night. The suns go down. Two hundred years go by. It's day.

She was right, though. It was cold here. Less so now. The twin stars of this system are maturing. They burn hotter in their old age.

A message comes through from the boss.

*How's Florence?*

*Fine,* I say. Four years go by. Four years, forty years, four hundred years go by.

Tina's coming back any year now.

How will I get her to stay this time? I pull out the brochure for this place. It's yellowed and crumbling. The marketing slogan for the planet is at the top: It's Livable! The picture shows a human woman and a male Xorbite. The Xorbite is pointing at his main lung with a tentacle, as if to say, I am really enjoying this nontoxic nitrogen-based atmosphere! The previous version of the brochure had the woman holding a fish, until someone's mother sued the tourism bureau for false advertising, claiming her son died because the picture misleadingly suggested it was possible to catch fish here. The dead boy's mother won and the bureau had to change the brochure or stop printing it, but since the bureau has no funding, instead of retaking the picture, the bureau just touched it up so that the woman now appears to be holding a football (or possibly a pizza) in one hand and giving the Xorbite a thumbs-up with the other. The happily breathing Xorbite is giving her a tentacles-up sign in return.

*

In terms of size, this is a Class S-4 Small World. Which means from up here, on top of the mountain, I can see the curvature of the horizon. A large cloud might cover a third of the sky.

Four years go by.

It's night. It will last a while.

The suns are setting, one on top of the other. The moons slowly reveal themselves, red, green, orange, and silver. It's not cold, but I know why Tina thought it was. The entire world is covered in cobalt blue dust. It's blue, blue, blue.

Four years go by. Four years, forty years, four hundred years go by.

*

A message comes through from the boss.

*What is the nature of where?*

I ignore that. No doubt hitting the Q-Grovoyoobian pipe.

*What is where? Where is when?*

Four years go by.

A faraway star implodes.

Something happens. Somewhere.

My aunt moves into the galaxy. Aunt Betty. She never married. My boss used to think she was a looker.

I ask my boss: *Do you remember my aunt Betty?* His high should have worn off by now.

Four years go by.

Aunt Betty was the smartest of my mother's three sisters. Unbelievably shy.

Her parents, my mother, friends, cousins, everyone tried to help her out of her shell, but that only made her crawl farther away from the opening, deeper into the cavernous interior of herself. She read constantly, kept her eyes down, wrote furiously in a journal. She was smarter than all of us combined. When I first got here, I thought of her, how she could help me figure out Florence.

Then she turned one thousand and everyone tried to set her up with someone. But there are only so many men left. Forty-seven, to be exact. Not a lot of nonrelatives to choose from. She moved away.

And now she's back. She got to that age where she wanted to be near family. Not with family. But near it. I guess I'm family.

*

A message comes through from the boss.

*Ah, yes, your aunt Betty. What is the nature of Aunt Betty?*

I guess the groovy yooby hasn't worn off yet.

I type: *Aunt Betty is a Presbyterian. Is that what you mean?*

Christians in the year A.D. 1,002,006 are few and far between. A lot of people don't even know what they are. Mainly because there are hardly any people left. Also, most of us stopped believing in God after black hole XR-97-1D got so massive it started swallowing itself over and over again in a recursive loop—like some cosmic Escher print—resulting in an object ten times the mass of the rest of the known universe. Personally, that did it for me.

Aunt Betty is constantly praying for someone. Her eyes are watching the heavens, expectant, as if it could be any moment now. Any moment now.

My question for her would be, now that we're spread out all over like this, one human to a planet, which one will He show up on? Will He pick one? Will He—in some mysterious way, the mechanics of which are incomprehensible to our finite minds—appear simultaneously on every world on which there are humans? How about the nonhumans? None of them are members of the flock, but when it happens, will they know, too? A Jehovah's Witness once showed up on a nearby moon and beamed me. I waited underground until he went away. Twenty years I waited.

Four years go by.

A message comes through from the boss.

*I wrote a poem for you. Do you want to read it?*

I don't want to read it.

Four years go by. Eighteen years, seven months, five days, ten hours, thirty-six minutes, and twenty-two seconds go by. Tina is supposed to be here.

Tina's not here.

It's night. It's day.

It's time for Tina to be here, but she's not here.

Something's wrong. She must have hit something. An asteroid. The Gheymu-mu-mut Belt is a minefield. She was probably tired and got a little careless and got herself nicked by a space rock, sending her ship spinning into another rock, and then it was pinball and she was caroming off asteroids. Or she ran out of fuel between galaxies and she's out there, floating in nothing.

A message comes through from the boss.
*Where is here? What is there?*
Four years go by.
Where is Tina?

It's night. It's day. It's the night of nights. On the night of nights, all the suns go down, and then all the moons go down, too. The whole world goes dark.
Tina is supposed to be here.
A message comes through from the boss.
*Question: When is where?*
*Answer: Not there.*
The boss is losing it. I log off for a while.
Four more years. Tina's not here. Question: Where is Tina?
Answer: Not here.

✻

The night of nights is ending. The suns are coming back up.

I had set it all up. I had candles on the table and a meal, a place for Tina and a place for me and chicken cacciatore and a salad, some spinach leaves and nuts and olives I found in the deep freeze, and a bottle of red wine. I had the chairs set up so we could watch Florence in the subsurface control room.

The blips are blipping.

A nearby asteroid disintegrates. Matter turns into energy; a ripple fans out into the fabric of space-time. For an instant everything in the universe wobbles. Then, with an infinitesimal wiggle, all of Creation slides back into place.

A lot of years go by. I stop counting.

It's night. It's day.
A message comes through from Tina.

*I'm sorry. I hope you are okay. I've left the fish on the far side of your moon, the nearest one, for you to retrieve when you have a chance. Give my best to Florence. And go visit your aunt.*

*P.S. I don't know any other way to say this without sounding insensitive, but I think you should know.*

*Your boss is dead.*

She's lying, I think, she has to be lying. No, she's right and I am the last to know. No, she's lying. Why am I always the last to know? I drink the wine straight out

of the bottle and put spinach leaves in my mouth.
Florence swims toward me. She's still a mile away, but
I can already see her eyes, her six-foot eyes, staring
blankly at a point an infinite distance behind my head.

I log back on. A message comes through from the boss.
*How's Florence? Good.*
Four years go by. Another message.
*Velocity? Radius? Stable?*
*Good. Good. Good.*

A message comes through from the boss.

*Good. Good. Good. Good. Good. Good. Good.*
Four years go by.
A message comes through from the boss.

*I'm so lonely. I've loved you for a million years. You've never seen me.*
*You never will. What is where? Who is how?*

❋

Fishing around in the storage cabinet above my
console, I find the module I'm looking for. It's in the
back, dusty. I've never used it before. On the sleeve,
in bright pink lettering, is the title, "Is My Friend/
Relative Actually Dead?" I put it in and watch.

The host comes out in a black suit. There is stock
footage of the universe. The Narpathian Falls look
majestic—one immense waterfall dominating an entire

planet. The Great Ice Plains of Farloooofarcha: a world encased in a solid layer of ice ten miles deep. People stopped in their tracks. Cars, jets, birds, balloons frozen in an instant. Preserved until the nearest star goes red giant and melts it. What will happen? Will everyone wake up and go back to their lives?

The tape tells me to pull out the quick reference card. Is My _____boss_____ Actually Dead?

1. Distance has gotten so great that it is impossible to verify whether your loved ones or other people with whom you are in frequent contact are alive or dead.
2. Most of the commercial systems out there use an artificial intelligence program called a logic-plus-intuition engine, or LPI.
3. The way an LPI works is this:
     a. You don't need to know how an LPI works.
     b. You wouldn't understand anyway.
4. Just go deep down inside yourself and ask one question.
5. Is he or she dead?
6. Remember, go deep down.
7. Deeper.
8. Even deeper.

I throw the card in the trash. I eject the tape and throw it in the trash, too.

A message comes through from the boss.

It's a video message. I have never seen the boss before.

There he is, in all his glory. He's balding.

He starts by taking off his shirt and his tie, then his pants, everything. He's bigger than I imagined, and softer, with a pale pink, nearly hairless torso like a baby's. He's talking to me. *How are you? I mean, how are you really? I'm so lonely.* He jumps up onto his chair. And now he's singing to me.

I don't want to ask myself. I don't want to go deep down.

❋

Four years go by. The boss is still singing. Or he sang. Present tense or past, I don't know. He's a recording, but he's always been a recording. Everyone is a recording to everyone else, a memory, a past transcript embedded in air or water or sound or light. No matter how close they are, they are not here. What they said, when they said it, it is not now.

I decide to write Tina a message. Just for kicks. It'll never get to her. Just for whatever.

I type: *You think you're too good for me.* I hit Send. It will never get to her. The universe will renew itself, collapse and expand and collapse and expand again before this message finds her out there, in all of that space, all of that distance, a sea of meters, an ocean of impossibility. It will never get to her, I know. I should go visit my aunt Betty. I tell myself I will go visit my aunt Betty. Next year. Or the year after.

*

And then it's silent. It's silent for a long time.

*

Four years go by. Twenty thousand years go by. Florence is circling, not making a noise. It's so quiet. My whole life has been quiet. And now it's getting quieter. Every person in the universe I care about may be dead. And I wouldn't be able to tell. All I can hear is my breathing. And the occasional blip telling me Florence is still alive, still moving through the depths. I should go visit my aunt Betty. She sent another card. She sends one every so often. Years pass. It feels like a lot of them. Years, years, years.

*

I go deep down.

I ask myself:

Is he dead?

Is she dead?

Am I dead?

Four years go by. Florence is circling. It's day. It's

night. It's summer. It's winter. It's summer. It's day. It's a storm that lasts eight hundred years.

✳

Four thousand years go by.

A voice message from Tina comes through.

*Hey,* she says.

*Hey,* I say.

Four years.

*Hey,* she says.

*Hey,* I say.

*How's Florence?*

*Is that really what you want to talk about?* I say. *For the last conversation we'll ever have?*
*Don't.*
*Don't what?*
*Don't be mad at me.*
*Okay.*
*No, really. You have to try not to be mad.*

*I thought you were coming here.* The harder I try to hide the self-pity in my voice, the worse it sounds.

Silence. Tina says nothing. Above the hiss and crackle of cosmic background radiation, I can still hear the boss. He has stopped singing. He says: *Here is just a special case of there. All heres are really theres.*

*I really miss you,* Tina says.

*No, you don't. If you did, you'd be here. You wouldn't be there.*

*What's the difference if I'm here or there?*

*Now you sound like my boss,* I say. The boss has started singing again.

*He knows what he's talking about.*

*Tina, he's dead. And in love with me. And crooning in the nude.*

*Why do you always want us to be . . .*

*Closer?*

*Yeah. How close is close? How close is enough?*

*Close enough for us to breathe the same air.*

*We're breathing the same air now.*

*You know what I mean, Tina.*

*Well, at some point some of the molecules of the air you're breathing* were probably in my lungs. *Eventually we'll breathe the same air, drink the same water, pass the same molecules through our bodies. Eventually.*

*You know what I mean. In the same room.*

*What's the difference? Anyway, we are in the same room now. A room the size of this galaxy. Why not a room the size of everything? Four walls around the cosmos.*

The boss is still going at it. He's scrubbed, he's smooth, he's nude. He's singing.
"I've Got the World on a String." "Fly Me to the Moon."
Florence is circling.
*But I can't see you,* I say.
*You can't see me.*

*Right. I think of being together as being able to see you.*

*Is it all a question of optics, then? Of biomechanics? Of the properties of eyes? What if you could see an infinite distance? What if you could see as far as you wanted, an unbroken Euclidean line of sight, in any direction? What if you could see me right now, halfway across the galactic cluster, sitting at my desk, so long as nothing got in the way? Would that make us close?*

*Tina. Come on now.*

*No, answer me. What's close? What would be enough for you?*

*There are gaps. When we talk. Long gaps between everything we say to each other.*

*Delays are a fact. Gaps are a fact.*

*So it's time then. That's what this boils down to. You don't want to spend the time.*

*Everything has to have a cost associated with it. Everything has to cost something and time is the price mechanism for the universe. Time is not so difficult to understand. Time is not such a mystery.*

*Then what?*

Tina says: *It's distance. Distance equals rate times time. Distance is the mystery. You're there and I'm here.*

❋

Four years go by. A package arrives from Aunt Betty. Vitamins and a calendar and a new toothbrush. A pair of socks. A note. "No need to visit. I'm fine. Hope you can use these." This year. This year will be the year I visit her.

And then it's almost Christmas, and, once again, it's the night of nights. A sun goes down, and then the other. The moons go down. Everything goes down. The sky comes up. It's Christmas Eve. It's been one million something thousand something years since the birth of baby Jesus. I've lost track. Everyone's lost track. I bet even my aunt Betty has lost track.

A message comes through from the boss. It's a time-delay Christmas carol for me. Away in a manger, he

sang, he sings, the little Lord sleeps. It's the last
Christmas Eve for another seventeen thousand years.
From now until then, all Christmases will be scorching
and dry and red orange with the light of two suns.
After this, more than a hundred centuries of blistering
Christmas Days, fiery and interminable. But for now,
it's night and it feels like time has stopped.

Tina is out there somewhere, whatever that means, and
I am right here, whatever that means, and my boss is
nowhere but a song he sang some years ago, a song he
recorded for me about the baby Savior, a song he is
singing while dancing naked for me, his penis and
testicles flapping like a pink, gummy marsupial, a song
just now arriving, color and melody at the speed of
light. Florence is swimming toward me in her silent
arc, sweeping through the mute, dark, frigid,
motionless water, looking at me with those eyes, and I
wonder if I leave if she will be okay. I wonder if I were
ever to leave if she would even notice. I wonder if she
knows I am here, knows what I am, if she knows
anything at all. What is she doing here, out in space,
on a planet by herself, in an isolated pool of water, no
food, no mates, no connection to anything at all?
How long has she been here? What would she have
done if I had never found her? What is she? What is a
shark? Do I know anything about sharks? Do I know
anything about anything? I don't. My boss sang and
sings and will be singing for who knows how long. My
boss sang and the song is still coming, my aunt prayed
and I hope she's still praying.

Tina is moving away at the speed of light, and if only I could see across the room, if only I could see across the universe, I could watch her. Florence is circling. Another card from Aunt Betty. I have a stack of them in the corner of the control room. Four feet high. That's it. No more screwing around. I resolve to go see my aunt Betty. I open the card. It says: "Didn't want to trouble you. I know you have your own life. Wished I could have seen you, but I know you're busy. I'm going to the Yttang-67 Loop. I have an old grammar school friend there. I hope she remembers me. Take care. Your aunt Betty." I ignored her one day too long. I was going to go. I really was, but I ignored her and she gave up on me and she moved away. Four minutes go by. Four minutes, four minutes, four moments. Four milliseconds go by. It's official. Florence is another year older. I sing to her. Happy birthday, dear Florence. She swims in her circle. A nearby world explodes. Happy birthday to Florence and to the baby Jesus. I have a goose and a ham and beets and sparkling apple juice and a beer and then a couple more. Somewhere, sometime ago, or now, or in the future, Aunt Betty is praying for me. She prays, she prayed, she will pray. Me and my boss, we sing a little harmony, thousands of years apart. We sing, Florence circles. I cut the cake. I eat it. It's good. I get ready for bed. I brush my teeth. I hit the sack. Another world explodes. Something happens. Somewhere. Four years go by.

## ( Man of Quiet Desperation Goes on Short Vacation

Man, 46, at some point in his life, looks around and says, How did I get here? A quiet boy grown up into an even quieter man.

An October afternoon, a Sunday, a narrow one-story house.

A living room, a couch, some chairs. An accumulation of nouns and furniture.

An ordinary moment in an ordinary life.

He notices the woman sitting next to him, looking somewhat concerned.

"This is the story of our lives, isn't it," he asks. Not really a question.

"Yeah," she says.

"And you're my wife in this story."

The woman nods and smiles the saddest smile he has ever seen, a smile so sad that he realizes, for the first time, that all smiles are sad, and in the way she turns down the corners of her eyes when she smiles he can see that he has put her through a lot and that he will continue to put her through a lot, and she knows this, and she will never leave him.

"Yeah," she says.

"You love me very much," the man says.

"I do. Very much."

The way she says "very much" sounds like the truth. It's the truth like he has never heard the truth before. She doesn't mean it with sentiment or virtue, doesn't want credit in the big book of good deeds or bonus points toward Heaven. She doesn't regret it or begrudge him a single minute of her life. Her love for him is not something that can be changed—it's physics, not emotion: It's the atomic weight of radium. It is vast and it is exact. It is tender and finite and inexhaustible. Her love for him is a fact. Her love for him is a brutal fact about the world. "It's not enough for me, though," he goes on, getting the hang of it. "It's not enough, is it?"

"No," she says, "no, it's not," and he is going to ask her why, but he looks at her and he knows that she understands him better than he will ever understand himself, and for some reason, he understands that it works better that way, and he knows that even if she tried to explain it to him, he wouldn't understand.

"Is this how it always is?" he asks. But he has a strong feeling it is. Beginnings are easy, endings even easier. The hard part is the middle, and for Man of Quiet Desperation, it goes from middle to middle, it always goes from middle to middle to middle.

*The City*
Man, 46, is in the city. At some point in his life, looks around, thinks to himself, *All I do is look around and think to myself.*

*The Movies*
Man, 46, is at the movies.

At some point in his life, he looks around, says to himself:

"At what point in my life did I start saying things like *at some point in my life*?"

That's the problem right there, he thinks. He's always starting out with *at this point in my life, at some point in my life, my life up to this point.*

*The West*
Man of Quiet Desperation has come out west. Way out west, farther west than he ever thought he would be. The

mythical west. The sky is pitched over him like an infinite tent, and it's been frozen into a blue so cold it has turned three shades darker than black.

Just on the other side of the dry riverbed is the Land of the Imperfect Past Tense, of ghosts and romance. On the other side the story moves and flows and overlaps onto itself, a ribbon, a wave, a swirling cumulus of loss, while on this side he can only watch, watch and look, trapped in the static present, the desperate moment of right now, and right now, and right now.

*The City*
Man of Quiet Desperation is in the tired city. On the bus full of defeated strangers.

This is not the bus that takes you to new places. This is the bus that takes you home. The older woman who wears a tattered hat takes this bus. Up close, she smells like day-old urine. There is a permanent smile on her face, but after looking at it for a while, Man of Quiet Desperation sees that the woman isn't smiling at all. She has all of the ingredients, the technical requirements of a smile, the muscular contractions. But something is missing. Her smile frightens everyone on the bus but she does not stop smiling. He thinks he can make her stop, if he could only make her look at him, he would smile at her and she would see him and stop, but she won't look at him. She just keeps smiling. She smiles and smiles and smiles.

*The Motel Room*

Man of Quiet Desperation has a room at the roadside motel. This is the room where people go to say things they have never said. This is the room where prayers are spoken, in earnest, by the sink, in front of the leaky faucet, knees on the grime-covered floor tiles, faces flush with alcoholic heat pressed against the cold porcelain. This is the room with an ashtray, a television suspended from the ceiling, a drape that hides the sun and stores the lingering odors of what happened the night before.

He calls the front desk. The stringy-haired girl-woman picks up, talks low and close to the phone, as if preparing to tell a secret, as if everything might be a secret.

"I'm in *The Motel Room*," he says.

"Of course," she says.

"How do you know?"

"You're the Man of Quiet Desperation."

"What do you think I should do?" he asks her.

The stringy-haired girl breathes into the phone. "Stop running," she says. But he can't stop.

*The West*

Man of Quiet Desperation is back in the west. In the

middle of the night, a noise wakes him. He thinks he hears someone for a moment, but then the footfalls are softer and softer and then all he can hear is the fire and his sleeping horse. The fire is alive, a small creature with ambition and a plan. His horse exhales soft, warm, wet breaths into the still night air. Everything is a secret. Everything.

*The Movies*
Man of Quiet Desperation is inside the theater. It is very dark, darker than usual. It smells like rancid butter and smoke—someone has actually lit a cigar.

Onscreen, thin, well-dressed rich people mutter ambiguously hurtful things to each other.

He:  [something about the limits of language]
She:  That's always been true.
He:  [something about the nature of distance]
She:  What do you want from me?
He:  [something about the unknowability of the human heart/brain/soul]
She:  (sobs)
He:  (sobs)
She:  [something about his family, his nose]

*The Motel Room*
Man of Quiet Desperation is in the motel room. The sink is dripping. Someone calls on the phone and says, You don't have to be alone tonight. Through the drapes, Man, 46, can see the moon. The front desk calls and

says nothing, just listens to him lying there, breathing like a sleeping child.

In the middle of the night, the television wakes him up. It's a commercial for a magic pill. A pill that makes you feel better.

"This is for you," the television man says, mouthful of teeth and headful of hair. "It will help you stop running."

## The West

Man of Quiet Desperation is back out west. The allegorical west, where everything means something else. The horse is the man's weary heart. The sky is the duration of his life. The cold is the truth. The black storm cloud is the impossibility of consistency. The water frozen solid inside the flesh of the cloud is self-consciousness. The border is a map of desire. In the west, almost everything means something, but the Man of Quiet Desperation is a quiet, desperate man. Some things are just themselves.

## The Mostly Empty World

Man of Quiet Desperation is in the stark, barren landscape. A tree with no leaves shoots up from the otherwise featureless foreground. There is a low-hanging sun but no shadows. All of the objects around him he can count on his ten fingers. No one has bothered to fill in the details of this world. It is empty now, but before long the real world will leak in and he will have to move on.

### The Motel Room
Man of Quiet Desperation starts to realize something.

### The City
He does not realize something so much as he starts to almost realize something. It is a familiar feeling. He is always doing this. This is his job.

### The Movies
He is always getting into these situations where he is about to realize something and it isn't a nice feeling or a painful but good feeling, like tension inside accumulating and then suddenly being released from a hole on the top of his head.

### The Motel Room
It isn't a moment when his field and depth of vision suddenly expand or a goose-pimple-inducing thought of simplicity and certitude or a rule about the world or a breaking of a rule about the world suddenly occurs to him. It is a sick feeling. It makes him nauseated. It makes him want to vomit everything he has inside him and then continue to vomit, until only blood and bile and then even the tissues of his organs start to come up. The liquid in his stomach sloshes around and splashes up against the inside of him. That's how he knows he is on the verge of realizing something.

### The Bookstore
What is he starting to realize? And where does it come from? From up above? Down below? Certainly not

from inside, because what, if anything, ever happens like that? Maybe for other people. Maybe for geniuses. But he isn't a genius. Anyone who would buy a book entitled *Organize Your Days,* who would read a book called *Get a Life,* anyone who needs this kind of advice is not a genius. These are not books for geniuses. These are not books written by geniuses. These are books for people who have trouble with things you aren't even supposed to have trouble with. These are books for ordinary people, for the mass of men.

## The Dinner Party

The thought occurred to Man of Quiet Desperation, a thought of unknown origin, from somewhere above or outside, as if it were being narrated to him, planted inside his consciousness. Man of Quiet Desperation, with a sickening feeling in his gut, started to realize where he was.

## The West

And it occurs to him that things don't just occur to people, like in stories. People always know everything there is to know about themselves, never any less. Everything is a secret that everyone knows. A secret that no one knows they know. To smile is the greatest mystery possible, to smile is to tell a secret, is to tell a lie from your head and a truth from your heart together, in one word—the conjugation of the terrifying present, the perfect past, the conditional future all in a single wordless word in the eternal, tenseless grammar.

*You Can Never Go Home Again Because There Never Was a Home to Begin With*

Man, 46, at some point in his life, tries to go back to the house, back to where it all started, back to where it always starts. To see his wife. Maybe get to know her, maybe settle down.

When he walks through the door, he sees her, still sitting on the couch where he left her, ten minutes, ten days, ten thousand lifetimes ago.

"You waited," he says.

"You came back," she says.

"I can't stay long."

"I know."

"I have to get back to work," he says. She is crying. "Can you ever take a break?" she asks. "Maybe we could go somewhere for a long weekend, somewhere less stark. Sci-fi? How about a Messy Realism?" Anywhere, she says, I'll go anywhere with you.

But Man of Quiet Desperation is already at the door, putting on his coat, tying an old scarf twice around his neck.

*The Bookstore*

Man, 46, is going from story to story to story, from middle to middle, hoping for a break, some white space, an empty page, looking around, saying to himself, *At this point in my life, at this point in my life,* on the verge of a secret, of telling himself the secret he already knows: *At this point in his life is every point in his life.*

Man of Quiet Desperation keeps moving.

*The Party*
He is at the party—

*The West*
—and then in the mythical west—

*The City*
—and on the bus—

*The Movies*
—in the theater—

*The Motel Room*
—in the loneliest room—

*The Constant World*
—never stopping—the bar, the crowded restaurant, the church, the web of romantic intrigue, the awkward situation. He knows someone has to do it, but why does it have to be him? He is the Man of Quiet Desperation and this is what he does and he is okay just to keep doing it, for what they pay him, it's a living, it's an okay life, but sometimes he wonders if there might be something better somewhere, but he will not stop, is afraid to stop,

wants so bad to just stop running from place to place to place, never any beginnings, never any endings, but sometimes he wonders what if he could only find a space to breathe, some breathing room, what might happen if he could rest for a moment in a place in between, an unnamed moment, a second to catch up, to just think things through, if he should just stop moving, if he should just keep moving, if he could just, if he would just, if he could only

( 32.05864991%

In the field of study best known as emotional statistics, the word "maybe" is a term of art, meaning, when uttered by a woman to a man in the context of risk analysis and assessment in an environment of asymmetric imperfect information flow, i.e., pairing strategies of isolated individuals located in major metropolitan areas in early twenty-first-century northeastern America, i.e., dating, somewhere between 31 and 34%.

More specifically, when uttered by a woman to a man, when such man is capable of love but somewhat unclear in his idea of what love actually is and when such woman is perfectly aware of what love is, what it requires, and what it promises, and what it does not promise or fix or heal or even mean but despite or maybe because of such perfect awareness is incapable of allowing herself to be loved, "maybe" does not mean "probably" or "probably not" or anything vague or indeterminate. When "maybe" is used in this context, it means exactly 32.05864991%.

For instance, when Janine K. utters the word "maybe" to Ivan G. in response to his query regarding it's nice to see you here again and perhaps sometime maybe we could, perhaps Friday, how about Italian or maybe Chinese, and you don't have to say just how about maybe just think about it and perhaps I can call you?—such query taking place in the pasta and sauces aisle on an average Thursday after work, Janine K. wondering if Ivan G. is scheduling his grocery shopping to coincide with hers, and if so, if that is a good thing, and if not, if that is a good thing— she means "maybe" and is perfectly aware that "maybe" means nothing more and nothing less than 32.05864991%.

Unfortunately, for at least two different reasons, Ivan could have misunderstood Janine's use of the emotionally statistically precise word "maybe."

First, of course, is the fact that despite Janine saying "maybe" and Ivan hearing "maybe" and both words appearing to be that five-letter English word uniquely identified by the ordered sequence of letters "m," "a," "y," "b," and "e,"

Ivan could have been under the common misconception that what people refer to as English is one language when, of course, emotional statisticians have known for some time that "English" is actually two completely different languages, one spoken by women and the other by men, or one by men and the other by men, or one by women and the other by women—the point not being the genders of the speakers but rather the relative levels of desire in any two-person pairing of isolated individuals.

In other words, there is the language of the wanted and the language of the one doing the wanting, and the confusing thing is that they are exactly the same in terms of lexicographical content, grammatical structure, rules of punctuation, and even pronunciation. The difference is solely in meaning. Some words mean approximately the same thing (e.g., baseball, accordion, yes), while others mean quite opposite things (no, never), and still others have meaning in one English but not the other, and some words mean nothing in either language.

Thus "maybe" was spoken and "maybe" was heard, but "maybe" is one of the words that means quite different things in the two Englishes.

To Ivan, at this moment the relative desir-or, "maybe" is most likely a synonym of "probably" and also a synonym of "hopefully" and also "you are special" and also "yes." And also "be re-assured, the world is just as you have always suspected it to be, principally concerned with you." To Janine, as established, it means just over 32%.

So as Ivan watches Janine handle the rotini, the penne, the farfalle, stalling for time, looking down at her shoes and then looking up, when she finally says "maybe," the word sounds to Ivan like a musical note sung right into the center of his heart. Weeks or even months later, when his desire has subsided, the two Englishes will collapse back into one and Ivan will hear the actual word Janine said. But for an instant, "maybe" is the most clear and unambiguous sound Ivan G. has ever heard.

The whole way home he says "maybe" "maybe" "maybe" to himself, like a piano tuner at work, depressing the same key over and over again until it seems to vary slightly with each itera-tion, until the note starts to sound subtly dif-ferent, either because the string inside changes slightly or perhaps the world around it changes slightly at the moment the hammer strikes. Each time different connotations of the word emerge like secret frequencies revealed from a deep, rich vibrato. He takes a shower, smokes a cigarette, puts a pot of water on for farfalle, and the whole time he is making a song out of the one note.

The whole way home Janine thinks about heuristic bias, the tendency humans have to systematically under- or overestimate probabilities. Janine thinks that generally speaking, as Bayesian calculation devices go, humans are fairly clunky machines.

Of course, Janine doesn't think of these things in so many words. She just thinks about what Ivan must think his chances are (good, pretty good, pretty damn good) and what they really are (32.05864991%) and she wonders why men are such terrible emotional statisticians.

She wonders why bees can sense magnetic fields, why dogs can smell on your breath what you had for breakfast yesterday, why bats can navigate through sonar, why humans can't do any of this. She wonders why we can see only seven colors, can't hear very well, and, by animal standards, have noses that are the functional equivalents of decorative spangles. Why, instead of actual useful abilities, what humans get is an intuition about probabilities—risk, chances, outcomes. How we get by on our crippled senses and slow maximum running speed because, most of the time, we can make good guesses about which berries are good to eat and which are poison, which thin ice will crack under our weight, which predators are not to be disturbed.

And how the mental rules of thumb that normally serve us well in filtering vast amounts of information, allowing us to choose rationally between courses of action and take justified risks, often undermine us in subtle and crucial ways. Hence emotional statistics: the study of the probability of success in matching isolated individuals into pairs, defined as

the number of desirable outcomes

÷

all possible outcomes

The key concept here being *desirable, desired, desire.*

As Janine merges onto the freeway and assesses her chances of survival, she overestimates her likelihood of being mangled in a horrific accident. She overestimates her likelihood of hitting an infant placed, inexplicably, in the middle of the road. She overestimates her likelihood of having all four tires blow out at the same time. As she gets home and throws her keys in the basket by the phone and checks and deletes yet another message from her mother, she underestimates her likelihood of letting one more day slip by without returning that call. She underestimates the cumulative probability that this will cause her mother to die of heartbreak.

Ivan, on the other hand, is cooking and smoking and drinking a beer, all the while unwittingly succumbing to that insidious heuristic known by professionals in the field as *availability bias* and known to lay persons as *lying to yourself to get through the day.*

In other words:
Ivan: *If I can imagine it, it could happen.*
Janine: *If I've hoped for it, it won't happen.*

In the shower, Ivan is soaping up and looking down at his ample midsection, also known to lay persons as his big fat gut, which he is sucking in without even knowing it. He washes his right leg, and then his left, and then soaps up his arms, which he assesses to be no less than 90% as strong as they were twenty years ago, when he was the best varsity pole-vaulter at a small liberal arts college with a surprisingly good track-and-field program and no women half as interesting as Janine.

In the kitchen making dinner that evening, Janine does not think about Ivan. She thinks about her father and whether he will call tomorrow. She is not happy as she looks into the refrigerator at a plate of sliced salami, seven pink discs of marbled meat perfectly spaced in a crescent, as she arranged them herself the day before. She is not happy but she takes the plate and a box of wine anyway and heads for the couch. She polishes off the wine without managing to eat any of the salami. When she wakes up a few hours later, the first thing she does is think of all the ways in which the day will go wrong. She calculates the probability of catastrophic failure and gets out of bed anyway.

In the morning, Ivan wakes up and the first thing he thinks of is "maybe." Today, he thinks, I will find out what that means. He has two shirts left in the current dry-cleaning cycle and a pile of shirts on the floor and a pair of brand-new slacks with the tag still on that he doesn't want to touch for fear that any deviations from his normal routine will affect something that happens during the day and turn "maybe" into "no." In order to avoid disturbing whatever tension lines of cause and effect may be between him and Janine, he has to minimize perturbations in the system and allow chance to take him where it will. Ivan flips a quarter to decide whether he will wear the blue shirt with faint checks or the slate shirt with a button on the breast pocket. Heads is blue, tails is slate. He flips tails and doesn't like it, flips tails and doesn't like it, flips tails and doesn't like it. He wears the blue shirt anyway.

All day at work, Janine thinks of the day to come, what can and will go wrong, deferring relaxation for anxiety and then deferring anxiety itself for a kind of pre-anxiety.

All day at work, Ivan thinks of Janine. Maybe. He types the word on his screen, doodles it on a notepad, says it quietly to himself in the elevator. Maybe, maybe, maybe.

In the evening, Ivan calls Janine. He dials slowly, waiting a full stop between each digit.

1.

3. 2. 0.

5. 8. 6.

4. 9. 9. 1.

In the moment between the tone of the last digit being depressed and the first bell strike of the first ring, in that silent space when Ivan could hang up, Ivan tastes, for the first time since "maybe," that it might not work out for him, that he can still salvage the situation, delete the event of calling, keep the secret of his desire, in effect stop the coin in midair, freeze the dice in midbounce, keep the two Englishes as one, end the observation before it interferes with the measurement, preserve Schrödinger's half-cat, pull the string back, keep the numerator from falling into the denominator, keep the world from splitting into before and after, heads and tails, two possibilities and one actuality, before the universe knows there are desired outcomes and undesired outcomes and tells him what happens.

Which brings us to the actual reason Ivan has misunderstood Janine's highly technical use of the word "maybe." It is a problem beyond the reach of emotional statistics and more in the realm of another, yet to be discovered discipline.

Ivan thinks he wants Janine to say yes to a date with him. Ivan thinks he wants to call Janine, and to ask her on a date, and for Janine to weigh her choices and decide between Ivan and other men, Ivan and women, Ivan and no man or woman, Ivan and whatever's on television.

Ivan thinks he is awaiting the outcome of an event Z: what Janine will say to him after she picks up the phone.

What Ivan does not know, what Ivan could not possibly have known, is that Event Z depends on Event Y, which depends on Event X, and so on and so forth, until we get to Event A. And the outcome of Event A, which is what Ivan's really waiting for, is what Janine is waiting for, too.

Event A started ten years ago, when Janine was a junior at Lower Peninsula High School and she had braces and a crush on Brandon, sweeper on the boys' soccer team, who liked English class and so didn't really hang out with his teammates, instead choosing to read alone during lunch, which Janine noticed because she had just moved and started school at Lower Peninsula and also ate alone.

Event A goes like this: Around the time of the Halloween semiformal Sadie Hawkins dance, when Janine was working up the nerve to call Brandon, whose number she had cribbed from the bulletin board near the soccer coach's office, Janine's father, Mr. K., left for the weekend on business. This was routine: Mr. K. was in sales then and he often left for weeks on end without so much as a good-bye. Mrs. K. was madly in love with Mr. K. and called him every night on his cell phone at whatever roadside motel he was at, just to say good night. Janine liked to hear her father's voice and often dialed for her mother and said good night first before handing off the phone to Mrs. K.

Event A technically began when, on a clear, blue October night, just before Janine was going to call Brandon, she decided to call her father first. It was late on a Friday. The phone rang several times and then went to voice mail. And then Janine called again and again it was the same thing. Janine hung up and didn't say anything to her mother, who had been sitting in the next room and had figured out what had happened. Janine didn't call Brandon that night, or ever. Mother and daughter went to bed without a word to each other, too nervous, each not wanting to look the other in the eye.

That night Janine did not say her prayers and she did not drift off thinking about Brandon.

Janine and her mother lay awake in separate beds, in their own rooms, unaware that they were each waiting for Mr. K. to call. They didn't want to assume the worst. They didn't want to assume anything. There could have been any number of explanations for why Mr. K. did not answer the phone late on a Friday night: bathroom, outside for a smoke, taking a drive to relax, shower. There could have been any number of explanations except for the fact that Mr. K. had, in 2,143 previous calls, never not picked up the phone when Mrs. K or Janine called. In fact, he had never failed to pick up the phone on the first ring.

Janine didn't think about this. She just waited. At some point, she must have fallen asleep because she woke up to the smell of French toast and her mother calling to her to come down. Her father had not called. So the two women each pretended they had a busy day ahead of them, and Janine ate her breakfast quickly and practically ran out of the house, and Janine and her mother each went to a different park and waited, though neither of them said anything to the other about it. They waited the next day, too. And just like that, a weekend slipped by without Janine noticing that her life had been put on hold. She had not called Brandon, she had not done any homework, she had not talked to or even looked at her mother. Those things could wait until she found out where her father had been on Friday and Saturday nights.

And on Sunday evening, when Janine heard her father's car pulling into the driveway, sounding no different, no less devoted, no more adulterous than when it had left two days ago, Janine felt a huge tide of relief wash over her. She felt silly for having assumed the worst, embarrassed even. Ashamed.

But when Mr. K. gave Mrs. K. a hug but not a kiss, it all started again. Janine had never seen her father do that. Mrs. K. had never seen it either, and she waited for her husband to come back into the room and start laughing, and kiss her and explain that it was a joke, and also explain where he had been. But he didn't. Upstairs they could hear the shower and hear him singing.

Just like that, Event A on Friday got linked to Event B, and now Janine was waiting for two answers. One moment Janine was perfectly happy, anchored to the linear sequence of successes and failures, days beginning and ending. The next moment she was adrift, waiting for answers, waiting for outcomes. There was no big event. No deaths, no parent running away, no explosive argument. A non-event, actually. Just a missed phone call. Just however it happens that people stop living days and events start overlapping, start getting tied into each other. The decision of whether Janine was going to allow herself to feel okay with things was dependent on some event a few hours away. And day by day it got pushed back moment by moment until it was firmly rooted in the next day. A few events in a day, a few days in a row, a few months go by, and then it's seventeen years later. Event A, Event B, Events C, D, E, and so on until we get to Event Z, which is where Ivan comes in, wondering what "maybe" means, not knowing he's waiting on the outcome of a chain of events that started almost two decades ago. Ivan, having pushed the last digit in Janine's number, has no idea what he is tying himself into, as he waits by the phone for an answer.

The phone rings.

The first ring is an eruption, a breach of the silence that seems interminable. Janine wants to pull the cord from the wall so it will stop. Then the ring is over. Janine breathes heavily, hand on the receiver, hoping there are no more, hoping it will just go away.

The second ring. It seems louder than the first. Now Janine's reaction is the opposite—to pick it up, to answer it, to let Ivan know, to let the other side know, to let the world know that someone is waiting.

But why should she have to pick it up? Why should she be the outcome, the right half of the equation, the answer at the back of the statistics book, the coin uncovered on the back of someone's hand?

The third ring. Why does it have to be Janine who decides? Why can't she just pitch her lot in with his? Why not wait to see if the phone stops ringing? Why not wait to see what she will be forced to do if the phone just won't stop ringing?

The fourth, fifth, and sixth rings. Events EE, FF and GG.

Rings 7, 8, 9, 10. HH, II, JJ, KK.

Rings 11 through 100. All tied together, hanging in a web. This is what Ivan is waiting for when he calls, all of it, going back to that

Friday night when Janine sat, nervous about calling Brandon, waiting to hear her father's words of advice. Ivan could not have known this. Ivan could not have known the cutting edge of emotional statistical theory: the theory that there are ten billion universes out there, similar to ours, each containing an Ivan G. and a Janine K. Ten billion Janines wait by ten billion phones, ten billion Ivans hold ten billion receivers, with ten billion suns setting on ten billion Earths. In each universe, the phone rings. It rings and it rings and it rings. It rings.

Ivan could not have known the theory that explains what "maybe" means, that explains where the number 32.05864991% comes from. The theory that of these ten billion universes, there are 3,205,864,991 in which Janine picks up the phone and says yes. Yes, yes, yes: 3,000,000,000 in which she has already picked up, 205,000,000 in which they are happily flirting, 860,000 in which they are making plans for a date, 4,900 in which they are having dinner, 90 in which they are looking deep into each other's eyes, and one universe—one in ten billion, one alternate universe—in which they have fallen immediately and irreversibly in love. Of these ten billion universes, there are some kinds in which she says yes, allows herself to be loved, and some kinds in which she doesn't, and some kinds in which it is Ivan who does the loving, and some in which it isn't. She wonders if the phone might just ring forever. She waits to see which kind of universe they are in.

# ( Autobiographical Raw Material Unsuitable for the Mining of Fiction

*Chapter 1: Miscellaneous Intervals Involving My Mother*

The structure of a proper good-bye works like this: There is a designated moment of leaving and there is a fixed quantity of wistfulness and usually the latter runs out just as the former comes to pass, resulting in neatly packaged episodes that build up to moments of emotional resonance to be dissected upon later reflection, when the details have been forgotten and stories can be made up.

❋

*Some Notes on the Premature Good-bye*

Sometimes, however, before the moment of leaving but after the decision to leave, there is a brief span of time, ranging from a few seconds to several minutes, when I am no longer present in, yet not quite absent from, my mother's house.

What happens is that we run out of things to say to each

other, run out of ways to say I miss you and you mean everything to me and so on, and we end up just staring off into the backyard at the ivy plants and our rusting lawn chairs. What starts out as the longing for home weakens into longing for the idea of home, which erodes into longing for the sake of longing, which eventually exhausts itself.

We drift into different rooms. We wander around the house. We pretend to look for things. We pretend to forget things and sit around pretending to try to remember what we're pretending to look for. We even pretend to look for things and then realize we've actually lost them. This is how we waste our time together: minute by minute.

✼

*Some Titles of Stories I Would Like to Write Someday*

The Story of My Mother
My Mother: The Uncollected Stories
The Definitive Story of the Particular Sadness of My Mother

✼

2m 06s

Another source of waste: time spent thinking about lost time. It goes like this:

Every Sunday night at eight, when it is almost time for me to leave, I start to regret all the time I have wasted. Instead of talking to my mother, getting to know her, I have done nothing. Sat in front of the television. Looked through old baseball cards.

I start to think about lost time and this leads me to think about the fact that I am thinking about lost time, which leads me to realize that I will want it all back someday, all of which makes me start to regret the lost time spent thinking about lost time. Which leads me right back to where I started. And so on and so forth, until it's time for me to go.

❋

*Some Notes from the Seventeenth Draft of a Story Entitled "Tying My Shoelaces While My Mother Looks On"*

It takes, on average, eleven seconds for me to: (i) notice the untied shoelace, (ii) bend down, (iii) tie it, and (iv) check the knot on my other shoe for soundness. These eleven seconds are spent in silence.

Assuming one of my shoes comes untied approximately one out of every ten times I visit, in a typical year I spend an extra fifty-five seconds with my mother due to untied shoelaces.

❋

*(0m 11s)*

(I once had a dream in which I saw my whole life, past and future, spread out before me like a deck of playing cards fanned across a table. It was wondrous. There must have been millions, tens of millions, hundreds of millions of cards—my whole life—subdivided into slices of exactly eleven seconds. But the feeling of wonder quickly gave way to a sickening panic as I looked closer and realized each and every piece was incomplete, cut by some devious method, some demon algorithm, some perfectly evil genius, in such a way that no one card was a self-contained moment. Someone had managed it so that any single piece was completely worthless, a stretch of perfect insignificance that made no sense, gave no solace, offered no closure.)

✻

*Some Notes on the Equivalence of Time*

I woke from the dream, my shirt heavy with sweat, and I knew this: Someday all those thin and delicate cards, lined up in their unique and pristine order, will be scattered, once and for all. Every last bit of fine structure, every intricate local pattern, violently and permanently erased. Any apparent design revealed as illusory. The entirety of the sixty or seventy odd years I had been given to spend with my mother, to make her feel less alone, will have been wasted, spent cataloging, anatomizing, epiphanizing.

At that moment, nothing in the world seemed half as absurd as trying to turn a sliver of life into, of all things, a *short story*. Where there had been tantalizing promises, near-connections, ephemeral and minute narrative arcs, one day there will be just a massive pile of my life, my mother's life, our lives together, severed into countless eleven-second pieces.

It will probably happen in this house, with my mother and me and no one else to witness, or, if we're lucky, in a hospital, with a nurse and possibly even a doctor standing by. It will be a surprise, no matter when or where it happens. And when that deck gets reshuffled, in the chaos, in the maelstrom of flying cards, I might have time enough to grab just one card for keeping, one card to hold on to. If the cards are cut the way I think they will be, then the eleven seconds spent tying my shoe while my mother looks on will be as good as any.

*

As much as I wish it were true, it is just not the case that I am infinitely inconsolable—not only are my consolations finite, it's almost embarrassing how modest they are. Sustained melancholy is tiring. As much as I wish I could, I cannot make a story out of everything.

*

*Some Notes on the Practical Limits of Longing*

I used to think that every time I left my mother, it broke
her heart. The truth is, it doesn't really break either of
our hearts. I wish it did, but it doesn't. We are a family
of two, each of us alone in the world but for the other,
and yet leaving is somehow bearable. Too bearable. Un-
bearably bearable. It almost breaks my heart how bearable it is. But it doesn't, maybe because we both have
our own lives, lonely and quiet as they may be. Or
maybe because it just is not very practical to let our
hearts break, once a week, right on schedule. Whatever
the reason may be, the fact remains that it does not
break my mother's heart and it does not break my heart,
and that's almost enough to break my heart.

\*

*Some Notes I Try to Shoehorn into Every Story I Write*

All of my stories start out as uncarved blocks of time
and end up as (i) a finished sculpted figure and (ii) a
pile of leftover pieces. When I'm done cutting and
chipping and breaking, and for the first time step back
to look at what I've made, I am always disappointed.
The figure I've carved is never what I thought it would
be. What I thought was form is a twisted, grotesque
shape, and what I thought was rich particularity is no
more than an accumulation of idiosyncrasies, and what
I thought were bold lines turn out to be jagged edges.
Details that should be in the story are not, and details

that were necessary have been left out, and details of both kinds have been lost, wasted, misplaced forever, unexamined and unexplained.

❀

*Definition of Frictional Loss of Time from the System*

A secondary effect. An indirect source of lost fictional material. A by-product of the differing rhythms of (i) humans and (ii) the machines humans use to connect, record, and transport themselves. Physical constraints include maximum operating speeds and minimum latency periods. Waiting at stoplights, waiting in elevators, waiting for phones to be picked up. I have lost innumerable stories to these frictions, the miscellaneous seconds and minutes dissipating like heat.

❀

*57m 44s*

The first story I ever lost to the Premature Good-bye was at the airport, the day I left for medical school. After a long and tearful good-bye, it was announced over the PA that Flight 2011, offering nonstop service from LAX to Logan, had been delayed for an hour. My mother and I looked at each other, unsure of what to do. After so much hand-wringing and wishing for an extra minute with each other, here we were presented with an entire hour, out of thin air. It was slightly embarrassing to have so much time and nothing more to say. We sat silently in our chairs, and then, after a minute or two, I wandered over to the magazine stand to browse. My mother bought a candy bar and walked over to watch the planes taking off. When it was finally time to go, we parted amiably, like acquaintances. I said I'd call and she just nodded.

What started out as a moment of departure and loss, a potential short story, withered into a nonevent. It was not unlike what happens when two people who have just parted ways realize they are leaving in the same direction. Some people will turn to each other and give an awkward little chuckle, as in, ha-ha, we said good-bye but here we are, walking together.

Some people, however, for reasons that can't be explained, will continue to walk in the same direction, side by side, neither one acknowledging the other. It's as if some Designated Time of Leaving has occurred and can't be repeated.

❋

*Some General Notes on the Use of Particulars*

There are stories about other people's mothers that are well told, that I can relate to, see points of intersection, say to myself, once or twice or five times, *yes, yes, true, yes, that's right, mmhmm, yup.*

Then there are stories about other people's mothers

that are so well told that immediately after reading them, I go to my desk and throw away everything I am working on, in a fit of self-disgust.

\*

*Some Notes from the Preempted Stories File*

And then there are those stories, other people's stories about their mothers, that are so well told they have the alarming and uncomfortable effect of making the hairs on my neck stand up, of giving me goose bumps on my head. They make me sit up when I read them, repeatedly, obsessively flipping back the page to look at the name of the author, to stare at it as if to ask, *Who is this person who knows my own mother better than I do?* When I am reading these stories I want to stop, I need to stop, because each word is like a tiny injury, a sharp, angled blow to the edifice of my ego.

I want to stop but of course I cannot stop, I cannot do anything except continue reading, word for word for word, until I am gulping the words down in whole sentences, accumulating injuries. And at some point I realize I am mouthing the words as I read them, even before I read them, and I wonder, *How am I doing this?* and for an instant the thought occurs to me that this person must have stolen my brain waves or at least my hard disk but that reflexive suspicion is quickly replaced by the realization that abstract premises, that is, potential stories, exist independently of the would-be writers trying to capture them. Whereas I had seen this uncarved block, waiting to be worked on, but had passed, unsure of what to do with it, someone else had taken that block and broken it open, chipped away at it, chiseled it into individual words, feelings, moments, people. Someone has beaten me to the punch and I am left to find another way to tell the story of my mother.

❋

*Autobiographical Raw Material Unsuitable for the Mining of Fiction*

"The Definitive Story of the Particular Sadness of My Mother" sits on my desk, uncarved, shiny and untouched. I have no idea what it's supposed to look like when it's done. I don't even know where to begin.

This is the extent of what I know: It will be complicated. It will have to include:

— a hysterectomy,
— ovarian cysts,
— a middling job neither menial enough to be comic nor substantial enough to take seriously,
— three quiet, unmarried sisters, mysteries to each other and themselves,
— scattered friends who slipped into acquaintances as years went on,
— my father, who ran away and reportedly drank himself to death.

It will probably also have to include the day my father left. That he shaved, showered, ate breakfast, kissed my mother on the cheek, grabbed his briefcase, and went out the door. That we knew he wasn't coming back. How the kiss on the cheek gave it away, because he had never done that before. It will have to include the fact that before my father had reached the corner stop sign, my mother was in my room giving me a look that explained that we would never again utter his name. Not out loud, not to each other, not in the house.

It may also include the following: how I told myself that day that I would work hard, study hard, learn to write. That I would get good enough, steal enough from others, and someday make a story out of the random and arbitrary disasters of my mother's life. I would put the pieces in order for her—act one, act two, scene four, scene five—fill it all in with the right colors. The story of my mother should describe how we silently agreed that I was going to make sense of it all, sort out her life and come back one day and say, Look, this is why this happened and you did this much, and you were the most this, or the least this, and this mattered and so did this. It should explain that we both kept hope that there would come the time when we'd have some long stretch of hours, or days, or a week, to sit in a quiet room and I'd tell my mother the story of her life, recite it back to her, a new thing, show her where it was funny and who mattered. I'd show her the one story in the world in which she was the main character, because she was too tired to keep trying to do it herself. I came back from college and I went away again and came back again and moved back in and then moved out. The whole time I was collecting details, piecing them together in little clumps, here and there, starting to see the beginnings of a plot.

Then one day I woke up and my mother had gotten old. And I had become not so young. And I went to my desk to look at the story and there were hundreds of new pieces, a secret store of senseless hurts, routine indignities, pointless hours. All of my work, all of the partial narratives I had been pasting and stapling and forcing together, it was all junk. "The Story of My Mother" had to include more fragments, more ingredients, more random intervals than I had ever imagined. And right then and there, I realized for the first time that I was not good enough to write it, realized that it was quite possible I would never be good enough, even if I had a thousand years. I realized that writing the story of my mother will require someone who can leave it all hanging, someone comfortable with ambiguity, someone with the ability to leave things out. I don't know how to do any of these things.

This is what I know how to do: cling to sentiment, collect the scraps, stockpile every last anonymous moment in my mother's anonymous existence. I've created a big box for it all and labeled it Miscellaneous. And in that box are millions of files, one for every unclassifiable moment in my mother's nonfictional life. Every eleven seconds a new file is created. I label it whatever seems appropriate. This is what I've settled for: the secret, deluded hope that someday, if I keep all these useless bits together and stare at them long enough, I'll figure out how to arrange them in just the right way.

## ( Acknowledgments

I would like to thank Frederick Barthelme, Mike Czyz-
niejewski, Karen Craigo, Mark Drew, Tom Dooley, Rie
Fortenberry, Ander Monson, Christina Thompson, and
Valerie Vogrin for publishing some of these stories, and
Carol Ann Fitzgerald for her encouragement, which has
meant more than she probably knows.

I am greatly indebted to my agent, Gary Heidt, for his
insight and for taking a chance on me, and to my edi-
tor, Stacia Decker, for her patience and intelligence.
Thank you to Sara Branch, Lynn Pierce, Jennifer Jack-
man, Jodie Hockensmith, Scott Piehl, and everyone
else at Harcourt for their efforts and for giving me this
opportunity.

Shout out to Mark Forrester for being a good friend
and an even better reader. Thank you to Rachel Sarnoff
for her enthusiasm and wit. Thank you to my brother,
Kelvin, for the lifelong conversation. And thank God
for my wife, Michelle, the funniest person I have ever
met.